CANCER

—Diseases and People—

CANCER

Steven I. Benowitz

Enslow Publishers, Inc.

40 Industrial Road   PO Box 38
Box 398   Aldershot
Berkeley Heights, NJ 07922   Hants GU12 6BP
USA   UK

http://www.enslow.com

Library of Congress Cataloging-in-Publication Data

Benowitz, Steven I.
    Cancer / Steven I. Benowitz.
        p. cm. — (Diseases and people)
    Includes bibliographical references and index.
    Summary: Discusses the history, symptoms, diagnosis, treatment,
prevention, and different kinds of cancer, as well as the possible impact
of research on the future.
    ISBN 0-7660-1181-X
    1. Cancer—Juvenile literature. [1. Cancer. 2. Diseases.]
I. Title. II. Series.
RC264.B46 1999
616.99'4—dc21   98-36123
                                                                CIP
                                                                AC

Printed in the United States of America

10 9 8 7 6 5 4 3 2 1

To Our Readers:
All Internet addresses in this book were active and appropriate when we went to press. Any
comments or suggestions can be sent by e-mail to Comments@enslow.com or to the address
on the back cover.

Illustration Credits: © Corel Corporation, pp. 86, 95; National Cancer Institute,
pp. 12, 17, 20, 28, 34, 40, 42, 55, 57, 59, 65, 68, 72, 90, 99, 106; Skjold
Photographs, p. 83.

Cover Illustration: National Cancer Institute

Contents

CANCER

What is cancer? Cancer is not just one disease but more than one hundred distinct diseases. It is characterized by the uncontrolled growth and spread of abnormal cells. Cancer involves genes, the chemical units that make up the biological blueprint of the body. Cancer begins because of many factors, including your own genetic makeup and environmental factors, as well as chance. Such factors lead to mistakes in the genes, which, in turn, can lead to cancer.

Who gets it? About 1.2 million Americans are diagnosed with cancer each year. About 560,000 die annually. In rare instances, cancer runs in a family. While anyone can get cancer, it is mostly a disease of old age.

How do you get it? There are many known ways to get cancer, and unfortunately, some are unknown. Smoking cigarettes contributes to about 30 percent of cancer deaths. Certain diets and environmental exposures may contribute to cancer, but scientists continue to debate how much or how little a role each may play. Scientists do know, however, that more than just one thing causes cancer.

What are the symptoms? According to the American Cancer Society, there are seven major warning signs of cancer. They include a change in bowel or bladder function, a sore that does not heal, unusual bleeding, a lump in the breast or testicle, indigestion, a change in a wart or mole, and a nagging cough or hoarseness. No one symptom means a person has cancer, but several of these, taken together, may mean that a person should see a doctor.

How is it treated? There are many ways to treat cancer. Often, doctors perform surgery to remove a cancerous tumor. The other two most common treatments include chemotherapy, which involves taking powerful drugs, and radiation. Both of these are aimed at destroying fast-growing cancer cells. These treatments are often taken together. Unfortunately, chemotherapy and radiation frequently damage healthy cells, too.

How can cancer be prevented? The best way to avoid getting cancer is to take certain precautions. Do not smoke, because smoking can lead to lung and throat cancers. Avoid staying in the sun too long, particularly unprotected. Sunburns can lead to skin cancer. Although no prevention method is foolproof, most physicians recommend a healthy lifestyle, which includes adequate exercise and a balanced diet of fruit, vegetables, and whole grains. A person should not wait for symptoms to occur but should go regularly for screenings and checkups.

1
Cancer: An Old Foe Begins to Reveal Its Secrets

The doctors said that five-year-old Abbey Steel had a cold or maybe hay fever. It was April in Virginia, and she had all the right symptoms: a runny nose and a puffy face. But when Abbey's parents got a call from her gymnastics teacher, who was worried when Abbey could not catch her breath, they took her to the hospital. Abbey did not have hay fever; she had cancer. The doctors said Abbey had acute lymphocytic leukemia (ALL), which is among the most common cancers that strike young people. They told Abbey and her parents that she had a fifty-fifty chance of beating her disease.

Abbey started on an intensive round of chemotherapy, taking drugs that kill fast-growing cells such as cancer cells. But chemotherapy also kills other cells, such as normal hair, bone marrow, and stomach-lining cells. Somehow, Abbey's spirits remained high. After she was diagnosed in 1988, she told her father that if she thought the cancer would "go away," it would. Abbey was lucky; after two and a half years of chemotherapy, her cancer did go away.[1] Still, Abbey, her family, and her doctors had to keep careful watch on the disease. One of the terrible aspects of cancer is that although a cancer may seem cured—its symptoms vanish and it is said to be in remission—sometimes it is not. Cancer can come back.

Abbey's case is an example of how far cancer research has come in the last several decades. In 1960, someone with Abbey's diagnosis usually was given three months to live. Today, roughly 75 percent of children with childhood leukemia are cured.[2]

Scientists are learning more and more about cancer all the time. This new knowledge is important, because nearly everyone has been touched by cancer. We know someone who has or has had the disease. It may be, for example, a grandmother, an uncle, or a friend's father. You may be a cancer survivor yourself. Cancer does not discriminate. Anyone—rich, poor, young, or old—can get cancer.

The word *cancer* conjures up visions of a long, often painful illness. It is difficult to treat and frequently involves surgery and sometimes extremely powerful drugs that drain a person's energy. Yet in recent years, cancer's image has begun to change, and we have many reasons to believe that cancer's secrets are beginning to be revealed.

The War on Cancer

In 1971, President Richard M. Nixon and the United States government formally declared war on cancer, deciding to put the country's vast resources into finding a cure. Nixon asked the nation's doctors and scientists to fight the battle in both the lab and the clinic. At the time, it was thought that all cancers could be cured. After all, Americans had landed on the moon just two years earlier. Little, it seemed, was beyond American know-how.

Well, the job turned out to be much harder than most politicians and some hopeful scientists thought. Many people did not appreciate just how very complex cancer is.[3] Slowly, through years of hard, long, frustrating research, scientists have learned more about how cancer works.

No two types of cancer are the same. Each type behaves differently. Cancer affects many different parts of the body, including organs as different as the liver, brain, and lungs. Some cancers affect areas such as the breasts and bones; others, such as leukemia and lymphoma, affect the blood.

Scientists have learned that cancer is a disease involving the genes. It results from changes in genes, the chemical instructions that control cell growth. Genes control which cells become skin cells and which become muscle, kidney, or heart cells. In cancer, normal cells, usually kept in check by certain growth-control genes, grow out of control.

Doctors and scientists are using their increased knowledge of the cancer cell to create new drugs that kill rapidly dividing cancer cells. Improved use of these drugs, combined

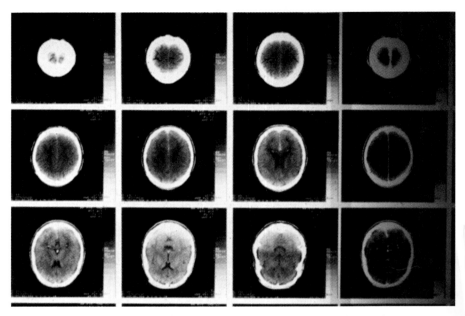

A CAT scan is just one of the latest methods doctors use to better diagnose patients with cancer. This CAT scan shows pictures of a brain.

with better surgical methods and more specific radiation treatments, are helping cancer patients live longer, healthier lives.

There have been some tiny triumphs in the war. Childhood leukemia is one example. Now most children are cured, and many can live normal lives. Hodgkin's disease, which affects the lymphatic system (a network of vessels, nodes, and organs, including the spleen and thymus, which make and store infection-fighting white blood cells called lymphocytes), has seen drastic improvements in survival rates thanks to new and improved drug therapies. New surgical techniques can often save patients from disfiguring surgery, particularly in breast cancer and cancer of the larynx, or voice box.

There has been other good news. In November 1996, the National Cancer Institute (NCI) announced that between 1991 and 1995, cancer death rates fell nearly 3 percent—the first such drop since records had been kept, beginning in the 1930s. Not only that, but in March 1998, federal officials announced that for the first time, the number of new cancer cases in the United States is declining. At the same time, the death rate from cancer slowed.[4] Some of the small victories are beginning to add up.

Researchers and epidemiologists—scientists who study the ways diseases develop in different populations—point to several different reasons for the slowing death rate. For one thing, cancers are being discovered and treated earlier, when chances are best for beating cancer. They note that more people are living longer, healthier lives as cancer survivors. More cancer survivors—some 8.5 million Americans—are alive today than at any other time in history.

Still, many people die from the disease. In 1998, the American Cancer Society (ACS) estimated that about 1.2 million people in the United States would develop cancer, and 560,000 would die of it. Cancer remains the nation's number two killer, second only to heart disease. According to the ACS, cancer accounts for one in every four deaths in the United States. One of every two men in this country is expected to develop cancer in his lifetime; for women, it is one in three.[5]

Not coincidentally, there has been a change in the way we regard cancer. It is no longer feared as an always-fatal disease, something people used to talk about in hushed tones. It is beginning to be seen as a manageable disease people can live with. Today, psychologists, social workers, and support groups are available to help patients and families understand cancer and how to live with it.

Although there have been many positive steps in the war on cancer, research still has a long way to go. In September 1994, the National Cancer Advisory Board, a group of expert advisors to the government, warned the United States Congress that the war on cancer had stalled. Critics have complained that despite the fact that more than 30 billion dollars has been spent since 1971 in the attempt to find cancer cures, little progress has been made in fighting the major killers: lung, breast, and colon cancers.[6]

Researchers believe that by understanding the biology of cancer—how and why it begins, and in many cases, how and why it spreads—they will be able to either prevent or treat the disease much better than they can today. They continue to explore how genetic damage can lead to disease. Still, despite all the amazing scientific advances of the past several decades, researchers face an uphill battle in translating those findings into new and better treatments. They remain hopeful, however, that more and more patients will lead normal, healthy lives in the years to come.

2

A History of Cancer

Cancer is as old as humanity itself, and perhaps older. The ancient Greek physician Hippocrates coined the term *carcinoma* from *karkinos*, the ancient Greek word for "crab." Possibly, he used this term because of the way a crab's legs spread out, similar to the way cancer can spread through the body. (Up to 90 percent of cancers are carcinomas, cancer that develops in the epithelial tissues.) Egyptian mummies show evidence that cancer afflicted people in ancient Egypt. Archeologists have even discovered tumors in Cretaceous-period dinosaur skeletons.

Cancer surgery dates back at least to 1600 B.C. Hieroglyphics, which is an ancient Egyptian form of writing, distinguish between benign (noncancerous) and malignant (cancerous) tumors. They describe surgery by Egyptian physicians to remove tumors with knives and red-hot irons. The doctors used compounds of barley, pigs' ears, and other ingredients to treat cancers of the stomach and uterus. These are the earliest known descriptions of cancer.[1]

Cancer was described hundreds of years later in ancient Greece and Rome by doctors such as Hippocrates and Galen. Hippocrates described disease in terms of four fluids: blood, phlegm, black bile, and yellow bile. People got sick if they had too much or too little of these substances. In cancer, said Hippocrates, the stomach and spleen produced too much black bile.[2] His theories, and those of Galen, who lived during the second century A.D., influenced medical practice for fifteen hundred years, into the sixteenth century. Both men believed cancer should be left alone.[3] Cancer was considered incurable, although some doctors combined a variety of pastes containing arsenic, which can be poisonous, in an attempt to treat it.[4]

Cancer in Modern Times

More than two hundred years later, signs of modern science began to take root. Two eighteenth-century French scientists, physician Jean Astruc and chemist Bernard Peyrilhe, conducted experiments that helped establish experimental oncology, the science of seeking better diagnoses, treatments, and understanding of cancer.

In 1775, London physician Percivall Pott first linked the environment to cancer. Pott noticed that young boys employed as chimney sweeps developed scrotal cancer in unusually high numbers. It was common practice at the time for young boys

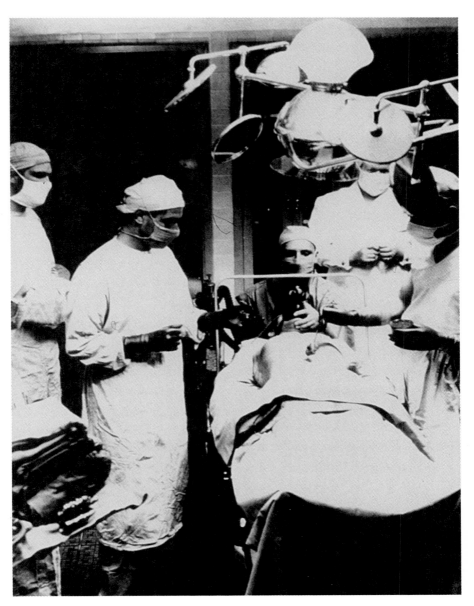

Surgery is one of the oldest forms of cancer treatment.

to clean chimneys naked. Yet it was not until 1915 that scientists actually proved chemicals could cause cancer.[5]

By the mid-nineteenth century, French and Italian researchers had found that women died from cancer more frequently than men and that the cancer death rate for both sexes was rising. They concluded that cancer incidence rose with age, was found less in the country than in the city, and that unmarried persons were more likely than married people to develop the disease.

In 1896, just a year after German physicist Wilhelm K. Roentgen discovered X rays, a breast cancer patient was treated with radiation. Radium and X rays were used to treat cancer early in the twentieth century, though early uses on humans were inconclusive. Animal tests soon showed that X rays could be effective in killing rapidly multiplying cells that make up cancer.

Understanding Cancer

By the beginning of World War II, in 1940, scientists had begun to understand much more about the structures, functions, and chemistry of living organisms. Better drugs were developed to fight infectious disease, and X rays were more commonly used to diagnose and treat cancer. Cancer research expanded as well, as scientists began to use improved research techniques, such as cell culture, a method to grow cancer cells to study them in the laboratory. They continued to document the effects of chemical carcinogens, substances that increase the risk of cancer. As doctors developed better methods to diagnose cancer and better treatment with anticancer drugs, the field of oncology became firmly established as an experimental science.

Scientists also began to find other things that could be involved in causing cancer. In 1911, Peyton Rous first found that a virus—later dubbed the Rous sarcoma virus—was present in chickens with cancer. In the 1970s, researchers showed that the virus carries a gene that can make a normal cell cancerous.

Changing Cancer Trends

As humankind advanced industrially and technologically in the nineteenth and twentieth centuries, the kinds and amounts of certain cancers people developed changed as well. While the cases of some cancers—cancers of the stomach, for example—declined dramatically in this country during this century, many other cancer types have increased in numbers. Cancers of the lung, breast, prostate, and colon have all become more frequent in countries where cigarette smoking, unhealthy diets, and exposure to certain chemicals at work and in the environment are common.[6]

Cancer was not as large a problem at the turn of the century as it is today because most people did not live long enough to get it. Many people died in childhood and those that survived usually did not live past the age of sixty. However, as many people began moving their homes from farms and the rural countryside to the city, life expectancy increased. In the city, with its better sanitation and improved health care, infectious disease, by far the leading cause of death, slowly began to decline.

At the same time, stomach cancer, once the leading cause of cancer death, became less frequent, thanks to safer methods of cooking and food preservation. Food stayed fresh longer and was less likely to spoil from bacteria. People were healthier and began to live longer. They began to die instead from diseases of old age: heart disease and cancer. Other changes occurred. Prior to the 1920s, lung cancer was a rare disease. As smoking became a favorite American habit, lung cancer, which takes decades to develop, began to appear.

Doctors began using radiation to treat cancer in the early 1900s. The first X-ray treatment room, pictured here, delivered radiation to patients after scientists found that X rays could kill rapidly growing cancer cells.

The Fight Begins

In the early twentieth century, as cancer started becoming more common, doctors seemed defenseless against the disease. Most people just avoided talking about it. Obituaries commonly left it out as a cause of death. Slowly, the public became aware of the disease. In 1913, the first article in a popular magazine discussing the signs and symptoms of cancer appeared in *Ladies Home Journal*: "What Can We Do About Cancer?" That same year, the American Society for the Control of Cancer was established. Its purpose was to educate the public about cancer.[7]

The public and many medical groups were concerned about the rising numbers of people getting cancer, and nationally organized efforts were getting started. The American Society for the Control of Cancer, for example, began to lobby Congress to do something about cancer. In 1937, President Franklin Roosevelt and Congress passed the National Cancer Institute Act, authorizing annual funding to support cancer research through the National Cancer Institute (NCI). Two years later, the institute was formed. Perhaps the most significant milestone in the recent history of cancer research occurred in 1971 with the announcement of the National Cancer Act. President Richard Nixon signed into law an investment of millions of dollars to support research to find a cancer cure by the end of the decade. Since then, about 30 billion dollars has been spent on cancer research.

In the meantime, scientists were busy at work. The first chemotherapeutic drugs were developed during the 1940s.[8]

21

In 1950, scientific research showed that people who smoked cigarettes were much more likely to develop lung cancer than those who did not smoke.[9] This announcement was an extremely important one, scientifically linking a very popular habit—smoking—to a deadly disease.

In 1964, the United States Surgeon General, pediatrician C. Everett Koop, issued a report concluding that cigarette smoking is dangerous to a person's health. Tobacco had been known and used in the New World before the time of Columbus and has been a favorite crop grown by American farmers for centuries. Tobacco use was long suspected to be a possible cause of cancer.[10]

Oncogenes Discovered

During the 1960s, scientists realized that cancer was a disease of the deoxyribonucleic acid (DNA), the master molecule in the nucleus of the cell that contains genetic information. One of DNA's most important duties is to control cell division, the process by which the cell copies itself and splits into two. Usually, cell division is closely regulated. But in cancer, the cell divides uncontrollably, pouring into surrounding tissue. In 1975, researchers led by J. Michael Bishop and Harold Varmus at the University of California, San Francisco, astonished fellow scientists by discovering that an altered gene, called an oncogene, caused cancer in chickens and was nearly identical to one in humans. This discovery led to the conclusion that cells can become cancerous because of the presence of an oncogene. It is difficult to know why some cells become cancerous, but some causes may be viruses, radiation, environmental poisons, altered genes inherited from parents, and, most likely, a combination of any of these.[11] Sometimes, though, the genetic changes leading to cancer have no apparent cause. Scientists dubbed the normal genes proto-oncogenes, meaning that they could become oncogenes, the genes involved in causing cancer.[12]

Though the chicken oncogene turned out to be restricted to mostly animal cancers, the work triggered a search for other normal genes that were altered in cancer. Three years after the Bishop-Varmus finding, Edward Scolnick, then an NCI scientist in Bethesda, Maryland, discovered an oncogene in rats. Skolnick called the gene RAS, an abbreviation of "rat sarcoma." A sarcoma is a cancer arising from connective tissue such as cartilage, bone, or muscle. Researchers eventually showed that the RAS gene in humans played a central role in as many as 30 percent of all cancers, including as many as half of all colon cancers.

Such genetic discoveries point the way for more milestones to come. Understanding the behavior of cancer is now tied to understanding the genetic changes behind its development.

Despite President Nixon's wrong projection, many scientists are convinced that the 1971 investment in cancer research is only now beginning to pay off, more than a quarter century later. For the first time since records have been kept, both the number of people getting cancer and the rate at which they are dying from cancer are dropping.

3

What Is Cancer?

Cancer is a group of diseases involving altered genes. It currently is the second leading cause of death in adults. All cancers have one feature in common: Cells grow out of control and often spread to other parts of the body. Once the cells grow out of control, they usually form a mass, also called a tumor.

In some cases, the tissue is a benign, or noncancerous, tumor. In other cases, the mass of tissue is a malignant tumor. Malignant tumor cells are different because they invade and destroy the surrounding healthy tissue. Malignant cells do not sit still in an organ or system. They can travel in the blood and lymph vessels throughout the body and settle somewhere else. This process is called metastasis. When a cancer spreads, it is said to metastasize. The cancer cells can then start new tumors in the newly affected area. Death results from cancer when the spreading cells are not stopped. They crowd out and replace healthy cells.

Though tumor cells may break off and form other tumors elsewhere in the body, the type of cancer remains identical to the original area of growth. When a cancer spreads from the colon to the liver, for example, it is still colon cancer. More precisely, it is metastatic colon cancer, meaning it has spread from the colon to other parts of the body.[1]

Different Cancers, Different Cells

Cancer comes in different varieties, depending on the location of the first tumor. A cancer is named for the area in which it develops. A sarcoma, for example, is a cancer that arises from connective tissue such as bone, cartilage, or muscle. A carcinoma is a cancer that develops in epithelial tissue, which lines the inside of the body's organs, such as the lungs, liver, breast, and colon. Skin is also epithelial tissue. Eighty to 90 percent of all cancers are carcinomas. Leukemias are cancers of the bone marrow and lymph system, which make blood. Lymphomas are cancers that develop in the lymph nodes, small organs of the immune system in which white and red blood cells are stored. The lymph nodes make infection-fighting white blood cells called lymphocytes. Hodgkin's disease is one kind of lymphoma; all others are called non-Hodgkin's lymphoma.[2]

Cancers are also classified by stage. Stage numbers describe how far a cancer may have spread in the body. Doctors need to know the stage of the disease to be able to decide how to treat it. Doctors usually group cancer cases into one of four stages:

Stage I cancers are small cancers that are usually curable because they remain in one place in the body. Stages II and III are usually cancers that are still mostly in one place, but have begun to spread, often to nearby lymph nodes. Stage IV is the worst kind of cancer to have. It is cancer that has spread far beyond the original area. It is usually so widespread that doctors may be unable to operate on the cancer. Drugs and radiation are often of little use.

Not Everything Causes Cancer

For decades now, the public has been bombarded with sometimes suspect claims that certain things in our environment cause cancer. This has led to an almost commonplace attitude among many people who, confused over reports in the newspaper and television, are not sure what to believe. Many pessimistically conclude that "everything causes cancer."

Of course, that notion is ridiculous. Yet the specific causes of most cancers are not known. Researchers know, however, that the top two causes—tobacco and a high-fat diet—account for nearly two thirds of all cancer deaths. Smoking cigarettes causes cancers of the lung, upper respiratory tract, esophagus, bladder, and pancreas and probably cancers of the stomach, liver, and kidney. Diet is often strongly linked to breast and colon cancers.[3]

Statistically, fewer than one of every ten smokers dies from lung cancer, so clearly, there are many factors that contribute to cancer. While research suggests that some people's genetic makeup may make them more likely than others to develop some cancers, most cancers seem to develop from a complex interplay of diet, lifestyle, environment, and chance.[4]

Why Does Cancer Develop?

One of the great mysteries about cancer is why it develops. Getting cancer is not that easy. Scientists know that cancer stems from a series of genetic changes. As cells divide in the body to make more cells, mistakes happen. Sometimes the mistakes occur in genes that control how cells reproduce. But people obviously do not get tumors all the time. Cells have an internal repair system that finds altered genes. The cell either repairs the altered gene, or the cell dies. In cancer, this fail-safe mechanism breaks down; cells either cannot recognize or cannot get rid of genetic mistakes.

Usually, within the body, certain cells—immune cells and skin cells, for example—live for a given amount of time, then die. Not in cancer. In many cases, researchers do not know why this normal process, called programmed cell death, does not work. Researchers believe that in about half of all cancers, a gene that helps control cell death breaks down, letting cells continue to grow out of control.

It Is in the Genes

In each of the body's billions of cells is a nucleus that contains the twenty-three pairs of chromosomes that carry the genetic formula of life. Chromosomes are long strands of DNA. Each

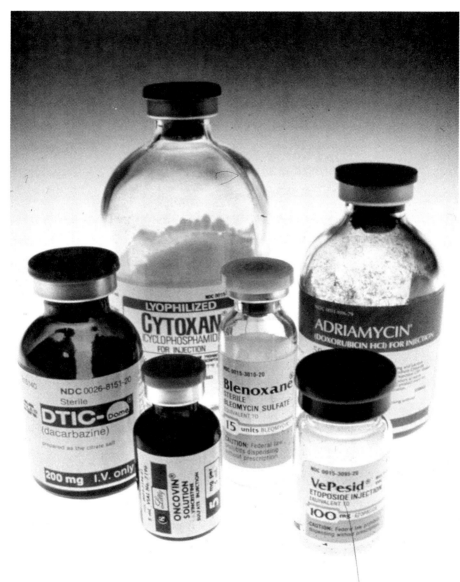

As researchers understand more about the genetic changes in the body during cancer, they are creating more specific and powerful drugs to stop the disease.

chromosome carries thousands of smaller segments of DNA called genes. In different types of cells, different sets of genes may be on or off. The ones that are on give instructions to particular cells to make a certain kind of protein. The on genes in a skin cell, for example, have the instructions for the cell to make skin proteins. The cell will have the properties of skin.[5]

Only a few hundred of the fifty-thousand-plus genes carry instructions for making proteins that control cell division. These are the genes involved in cancer. Scientists have identified at least twenty altered genes that can no longer control cell growth properly. Scientists think that in many cases these mistakes in genes reflect an accumulation of gene changes over a lifetime. Toxic substances—cigarette smoke, radiation, and others—can cause mistakes to occur in genes during normal cell division. Such changes in genes happen randomly all the time but are corrected before the cell divides again. When the repair genes fail or become less efficient with age, mistakes pile up. As the mistakes add up over years, they may eventually cause cancer.

Oncogenes and Tumor-Suppressor Genes

There are more than a hundred known genes involved in the development of cancer. Some, such as oncogenes, were once normal genes that turned on normal cell division at the right time. Other normal genes, such as tumor-suppressor genes, switch off the process. When they are working properly, both normal cell division genes and tumor-suppressor genes work as a team, enabling the body to carry out such necessary jobs as replacing dead cells or repairing malfunctioning ones. Alterations in these genes can disrupt these finely tuned systems. A cell containing an oncogene can be compared to a car with a stuck accelerator. When the oncogene is turned on, the cell will keep growing, dividing and making more copies of itself. A cell with a damaged tumor-suppressor gene is like a car without brakes. The tumor suppressor normally acts as a guardian, telling the cell when to stop dividing. Without this off switch, the cell continues to grow.

In cancer, both kinds of genes may malfunction. In fact, for some types of cancer such as colorectal, researchers

---

RAS

Rat sarcoma, RAS, is the most common oncogene. Approximately 20 to 30 percent of all human cancers involve an abnormal RAS gene. When RAS is altered, it goes into overdrive, making extremely large amounts of a protein, which drives cell division. RAS is like a relay switch in a chemical pathway that tells the cell when to divide. Normally, RAS is in the off position unless something turns it on. The abnormal RAS, however, acts like a switch stuck in the on position. It keeps telling the cell to divide, even when it should not. Scientists are beginning to understand the details of how RAS is made and are testing compounds that can turn off the protein switch.

---

know that oncogenes are turned on and tumor-suppressor genes are damaged. It takes a combination of several such malfunctioning genes and environmental causes for cancer to begin.

Still, genetic changes alone are not enough to cause life-threatening cancer. According to an accepted theory, most tumors will not grow beyond the size of a pea without blood vessels connecting the tumor to a blood supply.

Tumors produce substances that cause new blood vessels to grow, a process called angiogenesis. The new blood supply furnishes the tumor with needed oxygen and nutrients. It also provides a route for cancerous cells to break away from the original tumor site and travel to other parts of the body, where they may start new tumors. Some scientists believe that interfering with this process will someday prove a key way to prevent small tumors from growing.

What Causes Cancer?

Although carcinogens—chemicals, radiation, viruses, and bacteria, for example—may contribute to starting a cell on the path to becoming cancerous, scientists are not sure how dangerous each may be to any one person. In other words, certain chemicals may affect one person one way and another person completely differently. On the other hand, some carcinogens are extremely powerful and much more dangerous than others. Cigarette smoke is the most obvious and perhaps deadliest cancer-causing agent. Radiation from sunlight is another, causing almost all cases of skin cancer. But there are other good examples. High-energy radiation, called ionizing radiation, causes cancer as well. Studies of shipyard workers have revealed that asbestos caused many of them to develop lung disease. Secondhand smoke, or smoke inhaled from someone else smoking nearby, and radon, a radioactive, odorless, invisible gas that seeps into basements from underground sources, are other well-known carcinogens linked to thousands of deaths each year.

Hormones, chemicals that carry various messages in the body, can sometimes play a role in cancer. In fact, estrogen, which is an important female hormone that is responsible for, among other things, giving girls and women their female characteristics, sometimes actually encourages breast and other reproductive tumors to grow. Such hormone-dependent cancers are often treated with antihormone drugs that attempt to block the hormone's effects.

A well-known example of a hormone acting as a carcinogen is the case of diethylstilbestrol (DES), an artificial estrogen used to prevent miscarriages. It was banned in 1971 after it was linked to an unusual vaginal cancer in the daughters of women who took it.

Chemotherapy drugs used for a first cancer can actually cause a new second cancer. For example, the antiestrogen tamoxifen, which may prevent breast cancer in some women, has the possible side effect of causing uterine cancer in some older women. In rare instances some drugs used to treat Hodgkin's disease can cause acute leukemia.

Viruses and Bacteria

More than one hundred years ago, scientists began considering that viruses, bacteria, and other organisms might cause cancer. Proving their point was difficult, though, and only in the past twenty years have scientists shown that viruses, bacteria, and parasites cause perhaps as many as 15 percent of all cancer deaths. Few of these are in the United States; scientists estimate that about 5 percent of all cancers in this country are associated with some type of virus. However, it is very difficult to determine exactly how many cases of cancer and deaths are actually caused by viruses and bacteria because it usually takes a very long time for the disease to develop. Scientists are not sure how, but they do know that certain viruses contribute to altering a gene that triggers cancers to grow.

Only a few viruses by themselves actually cause cancer, though several are thought to contribute in some way. Nearly all cases of cervical cancers are now known to be associated with various kinds of human papillomavirus (HPV). Because of a widely used, accurate detection test called the Pap smear, which detects abnormalities in cervical fluid before the cancer has even developed, cervical cancer in women living in the United States is frequently detected early. However, in many developing countries that do not have access to such tests, it remains a public health problem.

Other viruses play important parts in cancer development. Those with hepatitis B virus (HBV) and/or hepatitis C virus (HCV), for example, have a greater risk of getting liver cancer. Both viruses can be acquired through blood transfusions,

Environmental hazards, such as chemical waste, may expose workers to material that may cause cancer.

shared needles, and, in the case of HBV, having sex with an infected person. Viruses—mainly hepatitis—contribute to as many as 80 percent of liver cancers around the world.

Human T-cell leukemia virus, a close cousin of the AIDS virus, is associated with a type of leukemia most often found in the Caribbean and Japan. The AIDS virus, HIV, is linked to a rare cancer, Kaposi's sarcoma, and to some types of lymphoma. Several types of cancer are suspected to be associated with Epstein-Barr virus (EBV), which is best known for causing mononucleosis. EBV contributes to about 50 percent of Hodgkin's disease cases and to 30 percent of cases of nasopharyngeal carcinoma, a cancer of the nose and throat that affects about eighty thousand people each year, mostly in southern China. EBV is believed to contribute to Burkitt's lymphoma, which is mainly a cancer of the lymphatic system, and is most common in hot and humid regions of Africa.

Only one type of bacteria—*Helicobacter pylori*—has been linked to cancer. *H. pylori* apparently promotes stomach cancer development in part because it causes stomach ulcers. Researchers continue to try to understand why infections sometimes are a risk factor for cancer in some people and not in others.[6] It is important to remember, though, that cancer is caused by many factors, not just a single virus or a single altered gene.

Diet

In the United States, scientists estimate that about 30 percent of cancers can be linked to diet. At the same time, many believe that as many as 30 percent of cancer deaths can be prevented by eating a proper diet. No one is sure exactly how what we eat and drink may actually lead to cancer.

Dietary fat may promote cancer by causing cells to divide improperly. Some fats are susceptible to production of free radicals, substances that are toxic and can damage genes. Sometimes that damage can contribute to cancer.

Tumor Suppressors

The first tumor-suppressor genes were discovered in the mid-1980s. Researchers studying a rare eye tumor called retinoblastoma learned that the disease developed because both copies of a normal, protective gene—a tumor suppressor, which prevents cancer from developing—were somehow turned off, damaged, or in some cases, simply missing.[7]

One tumor-suppressor gene, called p53, was discovered by Princeton University molecular biologist Arnold Levine. Scientists suspect that p53 may be damaged in 50 percent of all human cancers, including many colorectal, breast, and lung tumors. When it works correctly, p53 corrects genetic flaws that might be the first step toward cancer. When a cell's gene is changed, normal p53 tells the cell to slow down and stop growing and tells it to repair the damage. If the damage is too difficult to repair, p53 tells the cell to self-destruct.

But when p53 malfunctions, scientists believe, tumor cells are allowed to continue to grow unchecked.

Fat in the diet appears to be linked most closely with colon cancer. In most studies, red meat—beef, for example—seems to be a food connected with increasing the risk for colon cancer. Obesity has been linked to a higher risk of developing cancers of the endometrium (lining of the uterus), colon, and rectum, and possibly breast.

Cancer in the Family

A few cancers are inherited; they run in families. Usually, several immediate members of a family, such as sisters, brothers, parents, aunts, uncles, or grandparents, may be affected by the same type of cancer. Some people inherit a tendency toward a particular cancer.

Cancers that may be inherited include breast, ovarian, and colorectal cancers. Most cases of each of these cancers are not inherited, though. In 1993, scientists at Johns Hopkins Oncology Center, and separately at Harvard University and at the University of Vermont Medical Center, found a gene for an inherited type of colorectal cancer, hereditary nonpolyposis colorectal cancer (HNPCC). The gene's job, when it works properly, is to make sure that the cell's normal repair system is doing its job. When the gene is altered somehow, the system—called mismatch repair—fails to work. The result can be cancer.[8] Other inherited genetic changes can result in familial adenomatous polyposis, a condition that can lead to colorectal cancer.

Breast and ovarian cancers can also be inherited. In October 1994, a team of biologists and physicians in the

United States and Canada identified a tumor-suppressor gene, BRCA1 that, when altered significantly, increases the risk of breast and ovarian cancer. This finding was the result of an international hunt that began in 1990, after geneticists had located an altered gene by studying families that had a history of breast cancer.[9]

Only about 5 percent of breast cancers are caused by an inherited faulty gene. Hereditary breast cancer, however, may account for about 25 percent of breast cancers in women under the age of thirty.

4

Major Cancers

In the United States, major cancers include cancers of the lung, breast, colon, bladder, pancreas, bone marrow, skin, and reproductive organs (ovary, testicle, prostate, cervix, and uterus).

Lung Cancer

Lung cancer is the most common life-threatening cancer and the leading cause of cancer death in men and women in the United States. One third of all cancer deaths in the United States are related to tobacco use, and the majority of those are from lung cancer.

Many men began smoking in the 1940s, and by the 1960s, lung cancer was on its way to becoming an epidemic among men. The disease was a rarity among women. Men were six times as likely as women to die of lung cancer. Now the situation is changing. Lung cancer among men has been dropping since the 1980s. Women did not take up the cigarette-smoking habit until much later than men. As a result, the women's rate of lung cancer is climbing.[1] Today, more women die of lung cancer than of any other cancer.

Skin Cancer

Skin cancer is the most common cancer in the United States. Researchers estimate that one in five Americans who reach the age of sixty-five will develop a skin cancer. It also has the highest cure rate, approaching 100 percent if caught early. It is the most preventable cancer. More than 90 percent of cases are

Exposure to the sun without protection is the reason why there are more cases of skin cancer than any other cancer.

caused by too much sun exposure.[2] Those who are at highest risk live in areas that get a lot of sun, such as the Southwest, and those who are older than age fifty-five.

The two most common kinds of skin cancer—squamous and basal cell carcinoma—are easily cured. These cancers are marked by a sore or mole on the skin that changes in size, color, shape, or thickness.

The rarest—and deadliest—skin cancer is melanoma. Though it accounts for only 5 percent of skin cancers, its incidence is rising faster than any other cancer.

It usually takes at least ten to twenty years between exposure to the sun and the appearance of melanoma, though some lesions may change in only one to five years. Any change in an existing tan or brown area of the skin or in a mole indicates a possible melanoma. These changes include sudden growth, different colors, irregular borders, and a rough surface.

Breast Cancer

Aside from skin cancer, breast cancer is the most common type of cancer among women in the United States. One in every three cancers diagnosed is a breast cancer. Men can get breast cancer, too, though it is rare. About 180,000 new cases are diagnosed in the United States each year; about 44,000 people die from the disease. About 5 to 10 percent of all breast cancers are linked to a gene that triggers susceptibility to the disease.

The earliest sign of breast cancer is an abnormality detected by a mammogram, an X ray of the breast that looks for abnormalities in tissue. Such abnormalities may be spotted long before a most obvious warning of breast cancer: a lump in the breast.

Reproductive Cancers

CERVICAL CANCER

The cervix is the narrow outer end of a woman's uterus. Cervical cancer accounts for only 6 percent of all female cancers. Once Pap smears were introduced in the 1950s, cervical cancer was much more likely to be detected in its early and curable stage, particularly in women under fifty.

The number one cause of cancer is smoking cigarettes.

About 90 percent of all cervical cancers are thought to be associated with certain types of human papillomavirus (HPV), which can be sexually transmitted. Cervical cancer rarely causes symptoms in the early stages. However, abnormal bleeding or discharge may indicate cervical cancer.

UTERINE CANCER

The uterus is the organ in a woman where a fetus grows. Endometrial cancer, which is cancer of the lining of the uterus, is the most common female reproductive cancer. It accounts for about 13 percent of all cancers in women. If caught early, it is curable in 95 percent of cases.

The most common sign of uterine cancer is abnormal uterine bleeding. Other signs include pain in the pelvis, back, or legs; changes in bowel or bladder patterns; and weight loss.

OVARIAN CANCER

A woman's two ovaries produce eggs. Ovarian cancer is the second most common female reproductive cancer and the most deadly, primarily because it gives few warning signs. As a result, it is often detected too late. About 70 percent of women have advanced disease when diagnosed.

Some symptoms include abdominal pain, indigestion, pelvic pressure, loss of appetite, weight gain, and fatigue.

TESTICULAR CANCER

Scott Hamilton, winner of the 1984 Olympic gold medal in figure skating, was enjoying his career as a professional skater. In March 1997, he began to experience pain in his abdomen and a decreased appetite. After many tests, Hamilton was told

Childhood Cancers

Children's leukemias come in several types, a collection of acronyms such as ALL, AML, and CML. Acute lymphoblastic leukemia, or ALL, is the most common childhood leukemia, accounting for 80 percent of cases. Acute myelogenous leukemia (AML) and chronic myelogenous leukemia (CML) are less common forms of leukemia. Like all types of leukemia, they are diseases affecting specific types of blood cells.

Brain and other central nervous system tumors are the second most common childhood cancers, affecting from 3,000 to 3,500 young people a year in the United States. Brain tumors can occur at any age but are seen most often in children who are five to ten years old. Interestingly, about half of brain tumors turn out not to be cancerous.

Some of the more common solid tumors in young people include neuroblastoma, which arises from young nerve cells; Wilms' tumor, which originates from kidney cells; and osteosarcoma and Ewing's sarcoma, the most common bone malignancies. Other cancers include rhabdomyosarcoma, which develops in the muscles of the head, neck, and extremities, and retinoblastoma, a rare eye cancer. While Hodgkin's disease seldom occurs in children, the various non-Hodgkin's lymphomas make up about 7 to 10 percent of cancers in children.[3]

that he had a malignant tumor, twice the size of a grapefruit. He had testicular cancer. After chemotherapy and surgery, Hamilton is again enjoying a skating career. "My goal is to defeat this thing on every front," he said. "And now I've got to get back where I was. When I do that, I win."[4]

Testicular cancer is rare, yet it is the leading cancer among men ages fifteen to thirty-five. Fortunately, it is easily diagnosed, and it is effectively treated by combinations of chemotherapy drugs. It is usually cured.

The most common sign of testicular cancer is a painless lump on the testicle, or testicular swelling. Some men have abdominal pain.

Prostate Cancer

The prostate gland is a male organ at the base of the urethra, the duct that carries urine from the bladder. Prostate cancer is the second most common cancer and the second leading cause of death among men in the United States. It is the leading cause of cancer death in men over age fifty-five. In 1997, researchers expected more than 185,000 new cases of prostate cancer and an estimated 39,200 deaths caused by the disease. Some disease signs include frequent urination; painful, burning urination; blood in the urine; and pain in the lower back, hips, or thighs.

Colorectal Cancer

Colorectal cancer is the fourth most common cancer in the United States. The good news is that the total number of annual cases is starting to decline. Some experts believe that people are getting examined earlier, and colorectal cancer is being detected sooner.

Though its cause is unknown, at least eight different genes involved in its development have been identified. Many doctors and other health care specialists think that high-fiber diets help protect against the development of colorectal cancer. Still, this year, about 130,000 new cases will be diagnosed and about 55,000 people will die from the disease. Its main symptoms include blood in the stool and persistent diarrhea.

Pancreatic Cancer

Cancer of the pancreas, a large gland behind the stomach, is the ninth most common cancer. Because early symptoms are vague and no screening tests exist to detect it, it is difficult to diagnose early. As a result, the tumors have time to grow and spread. Only about 10 percent of cancers can be removed.

Signs of the disease include nausea and vomiting, loss of appetite, changes in bowel habits, and weight loss.

Bladder Cancer

Bladder cancer accounts for 7 percent of all cancers in men and 2 percent in women. Signs include occasional to frequent blood in the urine, which is rusty or deep red. This is the only symptom in 80 percent of people with the disease.

Brain Cancer

There are about fifty types of cancers of the central nervous system, which includes the brain and spine. About 15 percent arise in the spinal cord; the others develop within the brain. Brain cancers occur most frequently in children and the elderly.

People who develop brain cancer may have headaches, seizures, vomiting, and some changes in their personality and memory.

Leukemia and Hodgkin's Disease

Leukemias are cancers of the blood-forming system, including the bone marrow and lymphatic system. Bone marrow is the jellylike tissue that fills the inside of bones. Marrow produces three types of blood cells: red blood cells, which carry oxygen to tissue; platelets, which help stop bleeding; and white blood cells, which fight infection. Leukemias make up roughly 2 percent of all cancers.

Leukemia is the most common form of childhood cancer, yet it affects nine times as many adults as children. The two main kinds—acute and chronic—both affect the bone marrow. Acute leukemia is a faster-moving illness that disrupts the blood cells' ability to mature. In chronic leukemia, which may take longer to become a dangerous disease, mature blood cells do not work very well.

Leukemia's symptoms are vague. A person with leukemia is generally weak and pale, may be losing weight, and may tire easily. They may bruise often and bleed abnormally, especially from the gums. Those with the disease may have frequent infections and fever.

In comparison to leukemia, Hodgkin's disease is a rare cancer. It accounts for only 14 percent of all lymphomas and most often affects people in their late twenties. Researchers have greatly improved treatment and survival rates for those with Hodgkin's disease. Today, more than 80 percent live more than five years after diagnosis, which in many cases means that the disease will not come back.

Though some people with Hodgkin's disease have no symptoms, most may suffer from swollen lymph nodes, unexplained fever, tiredness, weight loss, and shortness of breath.[5]

Children's Cancers

Approximately nine thousand children in the United States under the age of nineteen will be diagnosed with cancer this year.[6] Some children will die of their cancer. Many more, however, will be cured. In fact, curing acute lymphocytic leukemia (ALL), the main type of childhood cancer, ranks as one of the major medical triumphs of the last two decades. Before 1970, fewer than 10 percent of children with this disease lived five years. About 75 percent of children who have ALL today will be cured.

Leukemia is one of two main groups of childhood cancers and the most common. The other main group, solid tumors, includes all the other kinds of cancers. The second most common childhood malignancy and most common solid tumor are cancer of the brain and central nervous system (CNS). Leukemia and CNS cancers make up approximately half of all childhood cancers.

The Geography of Cancer

The World Health Organization estimates that one half of all cancers occur in the industrialized one fifth of the world's population.[7]

Gastric and liver cancers continue to be the leading types of cancer outside the United States, particularly in underdeveloped nations.

The second leading cancer worldwide is lung cancer. As more Southeast Asian countries continue to pick up the smoking habit, lung cancer continues to grow globally. It continues to rise in American women, while dropping in men.

Cervical cancer is the most common cancer and the largest cause of cancer death among women in developing countries. However, in the developed world, it ranks only fifth in incidence and seventh as a cause of death.

Scientists have found that very often when people move from one country to another, the diseases of the new nation often affect them. For example, though it takes many years to occur, it is known that when women move to the United States from Japan, a country where women have lower rates for certain cancers than Americans, they begin to develop the same rates of cancers as American women. Researchers continue to explore the potential explanations, including differences in diet and environment.

Cancer in children is not the same as it is in adults. Children and adults usually do not get the same types of cancers. Children's cancers are derived from what are known as embryonal cells, baby cells that are still growing. The cells are immature. Children do not usually get cancers of mature tissues such as lung, prostate, breast, and colon, as do adults. If they do have similar kinds of diseases, the prognoses and treatments are often different.

There is also much less cancer in children than in adults. One reason is that some cancers can take as many as twenty years to develop. Also, children's cancers are often easier to treat, and young people are more likely to be cured. Childhood cancers have very few genetic alterations, because in many cancers such alterations need to accumulate over time. As a result, chemotherapy often works better in children than in adults. In fact, nearly 70 percent of children with cancer live five years after diagnosis. In adults, the percentage is about fifty.[8]

5

Diagnosing Cancer

Paul Wolkin was always an excellent driver. A Philadelphia attorney for many years, he frequently made the half-hour drive from his suburban home to the city. But one day in May 1995, he came home visibly shaken. He had had a car accident, sideswiping a parked car for no apparent reason. He tried to ignore it, but two weeks later, it happened again. This time it was even worse. When he tried to write his phone and license numbers on a piece of paper to leave on the parked car, he had difficulty writing the numbers clearly. Wolkin was seventy-eight, had always been in very good health, and was very active.[1]

Other things began to happen. Wolkin began to bump into walls while walking. He attended a legal conference in another state but had to return home early when he began having problems walking. His symptoms worsened.

Wolkin went to see a neurologist at the hospital of the University of Pennsylvania in Philadelphia. The doctor performed a needle biopsy on his brain. (A biopsy is the removal of a piece of tissue, which specialists later examine under a microscope.) Weeks went by before he and his family learned the awful truth. Wolkin had glioblastoma, the most common—and deadly—type of brain cancer.

Glioblastoma is a particularly hard tumor to treat. It tends to spread through the brain quickly and is difficult to reach and remove.

Wolkin had brain surgery and twenty-three rounds of radiation therapy to attempt to shrink the tumor. The doctors did all they could, but it was too late. He became more disoriented and began getting much weaker.[2] He died that November.

In Paul Wolkin's case, doctors had suspected that he might have had a tumor, but they needed to do many tests before being sure. When a person is sick, sometimes doctors can tell right away what the problem is. The diagnosis is obvious. At other times it is more difficult. In the case of cancer, many symptoms and signs resemble those of other conditions. Indigestion, for example, could be a sign of an ulcer or some other treatable stomach problem—not stomach cancer. Blood in the urine could come from a kidney infection rather than from kidney or bladder cancer. A flulike, hacking cough could be the symptom of an upper respiratory infection and have nothing to do with lung cancer.[3]

The American Cancer Society lists seven general warning signs for cancer:

- A change in bowel habits or bladder function

- A sore that does not heal

- Unusual bleeding or discharge

- Thickening, or a lump, in the breast, testicles, or elsewhere

- Indigestion or difficulty in swallowing

- Recent change in a wart or mole, such as bleeding or darkening

- A nagging cough or hoarseness [4]

These warning signs are good places to start in diagnosing cancer. Unfortunately, many cancers have no symptoms in the early stages. Much work is being done to find noninvasive tests for early-stage cancers. In this way, people will not need to wait to get medical attention until symptoms of late-stage disease show up.

In some cases, there are signals that something may be wrong, and it may be time to see a doctor. Generally, it is a good idea to see a doctor if the symptom has been bothersome for a while.

Most people have an idea of when and how often they move their bowels and how often they urinate, for example. A dramatic and prolonged change could be a sign of cancer. Chronic constipation or long-lasting diarrhea could be a symptom of colon cancer, as could blood in the bowel movement. Blood in the urine or painful urination could be signs of bladder, testicular, kidney, or prostate cancer.

Skin cancers may bleed frequently and heal poorly. Sometimes, people who chew tobacco or drink a lot of alcohol may develop sores that do not heal—and cancers of the mouth.

Tests for Cancer

When doctors attempt to diagnose a patient, they first need to know that person's medical history, including a list of current symptoms or illnesses, past illnesses, and the medical background of relatives. Doctors should also be aware of any medications a patient is taking and of anything unusual about the home and work environments, in addition to certain lifestyle habits, such as smoking. After completing a physical examination, doctors use the history and exam results to develop a list of possible diagnoses.

Doctors frequently order more than one laboratory test because a single test may not give all the information necessary to make a cancer diagnosis. Based on the results of the tests, they narrow the possible diagnoses and begin the appropriate treatment.

Screening Tests

Screening tests do not necessarily tell whether a person has cancer. Instead, they may indicate something wrong that may be caused by cancer—or something else. A screening test may suggest a condition that could lead to cancer. Mammograms are X rays of the breast that look for abnormalities in tissue. Chest X rays may be taken if lung cancer is suspected.[5]

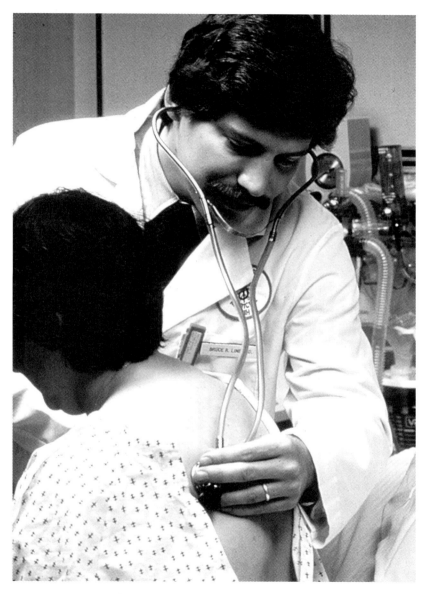

A patient's medical history, along with a thorough physical exam, will help a doctor develop a list of possible diagnoses.

Technology Improves

Techniques used to diagnose cancer have changed dramatically in the past decade. Technological improvements have enabled doctors to spot cancer earlier, a key to saving lives. For example, highly sensitive mammography uses X rays to allow doctors to see abnormalities in the breast and perhaps spot a growing breast cancer. Doctors today can use a flexible endoscope, a long tube that allows them to look inside the colon, to detect potential early signs of colon cancer. Computed tomography (CT) scans and magnetic resonance imaging (MRI) are other elaborate kinds of X rays that can be used to spot potential tumors throughout the body.[6]

One of the most successful screening tests is the Pap smear, which detects changes in the cells of the cervix, and has been very instrumental in preventing many cases of cervical cancer. In this test a physician removes cells from the cervix during a routine examination. Microscopic examination of these cells may reveal early changes associated with cancer. When detected early, cervical cancer is curable.

Some types of cancer, such as colon and prostate, can sometimes be detected by blood tests that measure levels of certain proteins. Abnormal amounts of prostate specific antigen, or PSA, may warn physicians of a developing prostate cancer. Rising levels of the protein CEA, carcinoembryonic antigen, may be a sign of colon cancer.

PSA testing, along with rectal exams, has become an integral part of diagnosing cancer. Since 1990, the number of new known cases of prostate cancer has more than tripled from fewer than one hundred thousand annually to more than three hundred thousand. The jump has been largely due to the introduction of PSA tests, which can find previously undetected cases of prostate cancer. By watching changes in the amount of the PSA protein in a man's blood over time, doctors can determine whether further tests might be necessary.

Monitoring is important, because usually the earlier a cancer is found, the more likely it can be treated successfully. Prostate cancer can be a dangerous disease; more than forty thousand men will die of it this year, making it the second

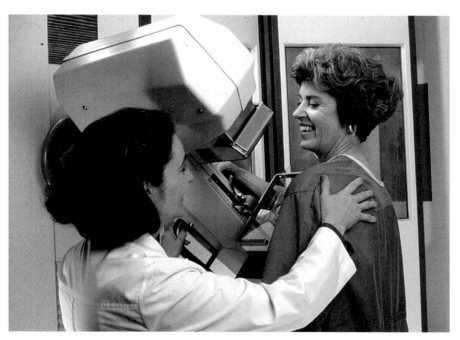

One way doctors can find out whether a woman has breast cancer is to use a special X-ray machine to perform a test called a mammogram.

leading cause of death among all cancers in men. Before the introduction of the PSA, two thirds of prostate cancers found had already spread beyond the prostate, making them nearly impossible to treat. Today, nearly two thirds of prostate cancers found in screening programs can be treated with surgery and cured.

But prostate screening with PSA is controversial, and many doctors question its value in some cases. Prostate cancer is frequently a cancer that men die with, not of. For many men, the disease progresses very slowly, much more slowly than other factors of aging that may eventually lead to death. For many men over seventy, most prostate tumors remain small and are unlikely to cause dangerous disease within a lifetime. Surgery may not be the best choice.[7]

Biopsy

When a screening test indicates that a tumor is present, a biopsy is next. A biopsy is the most accurate way to confirm the presence of cancer.[8] Surgeons remove a piece of tumor to examine it under a microscope. Trained specialists can then tell if the tumor is benign—noncancerous—or malignant, which means that cancer cells are present. If cancer is found, the biopsy may also provide information that can affect treatment.

During a biopsy, the tissue may be removed through a needle, an endoscope (a lighted, cylinder-shaped magnifying instrument), or by surgery. The biopsy may be done in the doctor's office, in an outpatient surgical facility while the patient is awake, or in a hospital under general anesthesia.

Much depends on where the suspected tumor is located, the amount of tissue involved, and the size of the tumor.

There are several types of biopsies. The simplest method is fine needle aspiration. Needle biopsies are usually performed on tumors that are easy to reach, such as breast cancer. They sometimes can be done on tumors of organs such as the pancreas or liver, which are deep in the body. In such cases, various kinds of imaging such as ultrasound or computed tomography (CT) imaging, which uses X rays and a computer to produce images of the body, may be needed to guide the needle to the proper place.

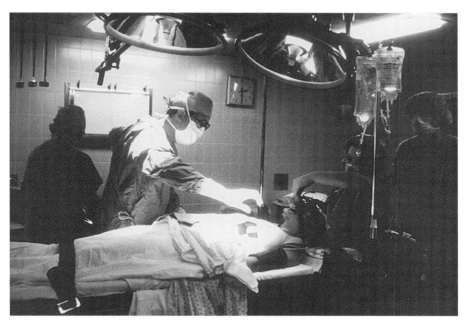

Doctors use a test called a biopsy to help confirm a diagnosis of cancer. They remove a tiny piece of tissue to test for cancer cells in the laboratory.

Removing suspicious tissue during surgery can be an expensive and risky biopsy method. But it allows more tissue to be removed more precisely than can be done by other methods. The more tissue the pathologist—the doctor who examines the tissue sample—has, the more definite he or she can be about a diagnosis. Surgeons may remove a piece of the tumor at first, and then if it is cancerous, remove the rest at a later time. They may also remove the entire tumor and some surrounding healthy tissue. The goal is both to get an accurate diagnosis and, it is hoped, to cure the disease.

Another way to peer deep within the body to diagnose a possible cancer is by using an endoscope. It is narrow enough to fit through various body openings, such as the nose, mouth, or through a small incision made almost anywhere. Surgeons can use the endoscope to remove tissue pieces for biopsy. Several different types exist. A colonoscope views the colon; a bronchoscope, the lungs.

Once doctors know what kind of cancer a patient suffers from, and how developed the disease is, they can decide on treatment.

Genetic Testing

For now, while some cancers seem to be hereditary, most cannot be screened through genetic tests. As researchers continue to understand the various genetic origins of different types of cancer, they will likely be able to devise tests to spot disease genes.

At present, only a few types of cancer—breast, ovarian, and colon, for example—have susceptibility tests. Such tests aim to find altered genes that may increase the likelihood of developing cancer. Researchers are homing in on others, such as genes involved in prostate cancer. But because only a small fraction of cases of these diseases are inherited, and many tests need to be improved, few doctors recommend genetic testing for the general population.

Many questions remain. It is important to remember that altered genes involved in hereditary cancers are signs of some increased risk. If a person carries an altered gene for a disease, that person has a greater likelihood of developing the disease. But increased likelihood is not certainty. The person may not get cancer.

6

Treating Cancer

racy Newhall knew the signs of breast cancer when she found a lump in her breast in August 1996. Still, the thirty-seven-year-old oncology nurse was shocked when she was diagnosed with breast cancer later that month. "I wanted to be around to see my four-year-old graduate high school," she recalled. "I had put in so much time helping others. I thought about a lot of patients that I had helped through chemotherapy. I didn't think it should happen to me." Newhall was scared.[1]

She volunteered to participate in a clinical trial, which is a study designed to test on human beings promising new forms of therapy that have shown anticancer effects in the laboratory or in animal experiments. After surgery to remove the cancerous tumor, she received both chemotherapy and radiation. The trial compared the effectiveness of standard drug therapy already used to treat the cancer to the experimental drug Taxol. "I want to do as much as I can to stop the cancer from coming back," said Newhall.

"It sounds funny, but it felt good to be on a clinical trial," she recalled. She was both helping herself and participating in a study that might find out more information about Taxol. This information might help others with cancer. "No one forced me to be on the trial," she pointed out. "I could have merely taken the standard therapy."[2]

A difficult part was telling her son, who giggled at first upon hearing that his mother's hair would fall out. The toughest part was seeing herself as a cancer patient. She never saw herself as a victim, she said.[3]

Newhall said, "Suddenly, I'm labeled a 'cancer survivor.' People ask me how I'm feeling with a slightly different tone of voice." The experience continues to strengthen her. "I think of it as empowering me to make changes in my life."[4]

Clinical trials are often good ways to find out if potentially new treatments actually work. The standard treatments for cancer traditionally have been surgery, chemotherapy, and radiation. Still, it is both difficult and sometimes frustrating to treat cancer. It is not as simple as taking an antibiotic to cure an infection. Cancer is much more complex.

Researchers, for example, have learned that few cancers develop and grow in exactly the same way or involve the same genes. Some cancers are fast-growing; others may take many years to develop into a problem. Treatments work differently on different people. The most important concept in cancer treatment is that surgery, radiation, and chemotherapy are combined to provide the most appropriate therapy for each individual case.

Surgery

Surgery is the oldest form of cancer treatment. If caught early, a cancerous tumor can be cut out by surgeons. They also usually remove a small region of healthy tissue surrounding the tumor to make sure no cancer cells remain in the immediate area. For many cancers, surgery remains the first and best treatment. More cancers are treated by surgery than by any other method, mostly because small cancers that can be removed are those that have stayed in one spot in the body and have not spread.

New surgical techniques involving tiny incisions and special instruments allow surgeons to see and operate precisely within a cancer patient's body. These methods should spare some patients the trauma of traditional recovery from extensive surgery.

New surgical techniques for treating osteosarcoma, a bone cancer, along with improved use of chemotherapy and radiation, have resulted in more patients' leaving the hospital with limbs intact. Previously, some patients would have to have a part of an arm or leg removed to stop the cancer from spreading. Patients treated for cancer of the larynx, or voice box, nearly always had to have part of it cut out, and lost their voice. But in the last twenty-five years, by combining surgery

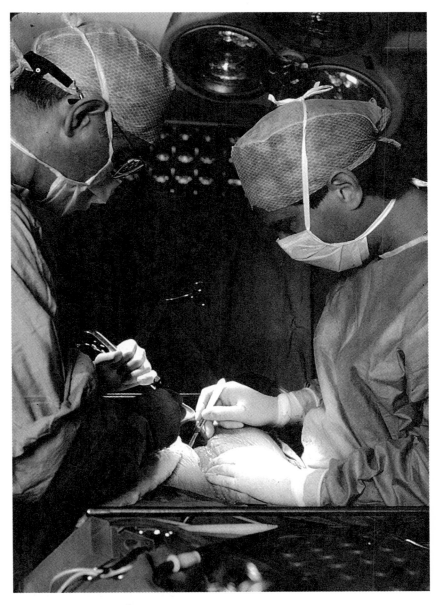

Surgeons remove a cancerous tumor.

with radiation and chemotherapy, doctors are saving more voices.

Changes in breast cancer treatment are among the most dramatic advances in the war on cancer. For years, women with breast cancer were more likely than not to have a mastectomy, an operation in which one or both breasts and the underlying chest wall muscle were cut away in hopes of getting rid of the cancer. But a long-term study conducted by the NCI from 1976 to 1984 showed that many women are candidates instead for a lumpectomy, in which a smaller portion of the breast, including the tumor and surrounding tissue, is removed. The surgery is usually followed by radiation to kill remaining cancer cells that the surgeon cannot see.

Other advances have made it possible to avoid colostomy—the surgical removal of a portion of the colon—as well.

Surgery is the key treatment for several other cancers, such as those of the skin, bladder, rectum, and stomach, and sarcomas. But because the operations have changed a great deal in the last twenty years—with the use of chemotherapy and radiation to shrink tumors—surgeons can save much of the tissue they were once forced to remove.

Some cancers can be treated by surgery alone. However, because surgeons cannot always see the entire cancer, chemotherapy with cell-killing drugs, or radiation are frequently given after surgery. This may reduce the chances that cancer will return after surgeons have removed all signs of the disease. Such therapy is called adjuvant, or additional, therapy. But chemotherapy is not a one-size-fits-all proposition.

Chemotherapy that works for colorectal cancer may not have any effect on breast cancer, and vice versa. Drugs that help one patient with prostate cancer may do little for someone else with the same diagnosis.

Chemotherapy

Doctors sometimes attempt to kill cancer cells by giving patients powerful drugs. The drugs attack the cancer, interfering with the cancer cells' ability to reproduce. These drugs are usually given intravenously, through a tiny, thin tube inserted into a vein. They may have side effects and frequently make patients sick in other ways. Most of today's treatments have a major limitation—they damage healthy cells as well as cancer cells. The goal for new drug development is to target only a patient's cancer cells, reducing the side effects. Drugs currently kill rapidly reproducing cells, which unfortunately include cells in hair, the stomach lining, and bone marrow. Many patients have nausea, and some lose their hair as a result of chemotherapy.

It is very difficult and expensive to develop new chemotherapy drugs. It may take many years and millions of dollars to find one compound out of thousands tested in the laboratory that may have some effect on cancer cells. Much of the success in chemotherapy treatment today has come from combining existing drugs in new ways. In many cases, however, drugs that work initially in combating a cancer ultimately lose their effectiveness. The tumor actually develops resistance to the drugs. A patient's best chance of beating a cancer, then,

Powerful cancer-killing drugs, known as chemotherapy, are usually given intravenously through long tubes that take the medication right into a patient's vein.

is with the first treatment. Chemotherapy is usually much less effective the second time around.

Today, 65 to 75 percent of cancer patients receive one or more powerful cancer-fighting drugs during some part of their treatment. The first chemotherapeutic drugs, developed during the 1940s, often were inadequate to fight cancer when given one at a time or even if given in a certain order. But in the 1960s, doctors discovered that they could cure some cancers if they gave several drugs at the same time.

Hodgkin's disease is an example of a success story for chemotherapy. Hodgkin's, a fairly rare disease (about five to six thousand new cases occur annually in the United States) of the lymphatic system, once killed two out of every three patients. Today, a combination of four different drugs can effectively wipe out the disease in several months in three out of four patients, even when it is spotted late. As with many cancers, the choice of treatment depends on how far along the disease is when it is discovered.

The Progress of Chemotherapy Drugs

Vaccines and antibiotics take advantage of differences between human cells and viruses and bacteria. But "cancer cells have the same basic biological machinery as do normal cells," noted Russell Schilder, a medical oncologist at the Fox Chase Cancer Center. Chemotherapy drugs, used to fight cancer cells, have problems telling the difference between cancer cells and healthy body cells. "Chemotherapy drugs are more toxic than antibiotics because they are killing normal cells. In fact, cells that line the gastrointestinal tract are fast-growing, and one of the reasons patients get mucositis [inflammation of the mucous lining] is because chemotherapy can't tell the difference [between cancer cells and normal cells]."[5]

Different cancer types are susceptible to different drugs. In fact, this led to some mistakes in drug testing in the 1960s. Researchers typically tested drugs against mouse tumors. If they were not effective, they were thrown away. "There were two wrong assumptions," said Schilder. "One, not all drugs active in human cancer work against mouse tumors. And drugs that might not work against one cancer type might just work against another, based on the biology of the cell."

Sometimes, after a drug is tailored to a particular disease, a menu of potential treatments is developed. Then doctors determine which drugs may work best against a particular cancer in a particular patient, with an eye on specific toxic side effects.

According to Schilder, government and industry research see the 1990s as a decade of new chemotherapy drug development, including such medicines as Taxol and gemcitabine. "None of these are home runs, having the impact of cisplatin [a now-classic chemotherapy drug used to treat several cancers] in the treatment of testicular cancer, for example. Many of these new drugs have little toxicity, so you can keep the patient on them longer, with better quality of life."[6]

Chemotherapy has achieved some of its most impressive gains against testicular cancer, the leading cancer of men ages fifteen to thirty-five. The illness temporarily felled Philadelphia Phillies baseball star John Kruk in 1995 and ice-skater Scott Hamilton in 1997. Platinum drugs, introduced in the mid-1970s, now cure a majority of testicular cancer patients. About 80 percent of men with testicular cancer that has spread throughout the body survive thanks to such drugs.[7]

Drugs are also used routinely to treat colon cancer, and about a third of breast cancer patients receive chemotherapy.

Radiation

Roughly 60 percent of cancer patients undergo radiation therapy at some point during their treatment. Radiation therapy uses high-energy radiation to kill cancer cells, to slow or stop the spread of cancer. Radiation has its greatest effect on tissues that divide rapidly. Cancer cells treated this way are left unable to divide and multiply, causing the tumor to shrink.

Radiation was first used to treat a cancer patient a little more than a century ago, just a short time after X rays were discovered by William Roentgen in 1895. Since then, radiation therapy has come a long way. Linear accelerators, machines that produce high energy in the form of gamma rays and electron beams, have been used to treat cancer for more than thirty years.

Today, a better understanding of how cancer cells behave has helped scientists design improved therapies and techniques. Better imaging testing such as CT scans and MRI helps radiation oncologists pinpoint the exact location of the tumor and treat only that area, saving healthy tissue. That is the goal in using radiation to treat cancer.

For example, in brachytherapy, a technique used to treat head and neck cancers as well as prostate cancer, doctors can insert a tiny rod with radioactive pellets near the tumor to shrink or kill it. The technique reduces radiation exposure to normal skin, muscle, and various organs.

When radiation travels varying distances, depending on where the tumor is located in the body, it may lose energy. Therapies such as stereotactic conformal therapy and the gamma knife use many radiation beams at the same time, allowing doctors to focus on the tumor, providing a lot of radiation to the cancer and little to healthy cells.

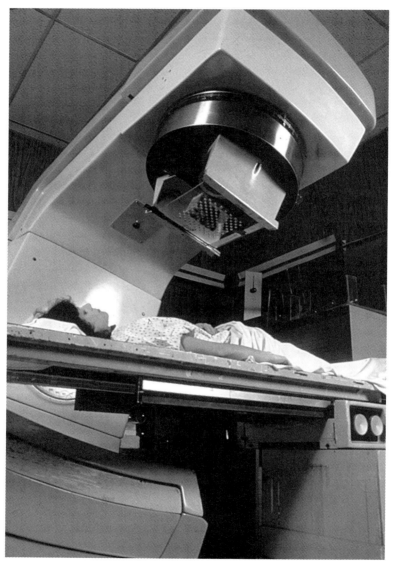

Radiation therapy is used for 60 percent of cancer patients. The high-energy radiation kills cancer cells.

While it is very difficult to eliminate all the risk to normal tissue, doctors are attempting to limit the risk by a technique called conformation radiotherapy. Using three-dimensional pictures of the tumor, doctors, with the aid of a computer, can pinpoint where radiation beams should be focused. Machines are now so precise that therapists can focus most of the radiation beam just on the tumor, lessening damage to normal tissue. Though some normal cells in the region of the radiation also are damaged, many cells can repair themselves within a few hours of treatment.

Sometimes the timing of radiation is important. In addition to cutting out a tumor, surgeons can help shrink it by giving radiation while the surgical area is still open. This technique is called intraoperative radiation.[8] While radiation is often given after surgery to kill any remaining tumor cells not removed during the operation, such therapy may sometimes be given before surgery to shrink the tumor to a manageable size. This is usually done when the tumor is too large to be easily removed.

Judy Besst, a nurse in Columbus, Ohio, was first diagnosed with breast cancer in 1981. When her doctors performed surgery to remove the cancerous breast that April, they found seventeen positive lymph nodes, meaning that the cancer had spread beyond its original site. She took chemotherapy for eighteen months and was fine until 1985 when she found another lump near her incision line. Doctors removed the lump after it was found to be malignant. Her doctors told her that radiation would be the best way to kill any possible remaining cells not discovered during surgery.

Besst had fifteen treatments in three weeks in 1985, and was cancer free until the summer of 1995. She began having chest pain and noticed some unusual swelling. Her doctors confirmed her worst fear—the cancer was back.

But Besst was confident about how far technology had come in the ten years since her last radiation treatment. She said she was not apprehensive when her doctor told her she would need more radiation treatment to fight this new cancer, which had spread to her sternum and lung. As she was completing her four-week therapy, she said, "The technology has come a lot further since I had my last radiation therapy, which worked so well that I remained tumor-free for 10 years. Knowing that the technology is even better now gives me hope that it will work as well this time."[9]

Immunotherapy

Immunotherapy, or biological therapy, harnesses the body's own defense system in hopes of defeating cancer. Physicians in the late 1800s became interested in using the immune system against cancer when they noticed that tumors sometimes shrank in patients with bacterial infections. Unlike conventional treatments, which attack the cancer directly, immunotherapy attempts to alter the body in such a way that its own defense mechanisms will reject and destroy the cancer. Such therapy relies on biologics, substances naturally produced by the body, which are collected from the patient and then modified and amplified in the lab, often using the modern techniques of biotechnology. The biologics are then returned to the patient and function in ways that go beyond the body's normal capabilities.

This process is not as straightforward as it sounds, however. Cancer somehow eludes the body's natural defenses because cancer cells are so much like normal cells. Cancer does not signal the immune system the same way bacteria or viruses do. Instead, the immune system is overwhelmed when the cancer grows too large or when it grows in a somewhat inaccessible area.

In fact, many biologics have worked successfully in the laboratory and in animal tests against cancer, only to fail in testing on human beings. There have been many disappointments. In the 1970s and 1980s, monoclonal antibodies were billed as the state-of-the-art treatment for cancer. Antibodies are cells made by the body's immune system to fight infection. When an infection occurs, antibodies are released in the bloodstream, ready to mark the invading virus for destruction.

Monoclonals are specialized proteins that, in theory, can seek out and bind to specific cancer cells. They either interfere with the cells' ability to divide and reproduce or directly destroy them. Monoclonals have not lived up to original expectations, however. In early trials, researchers discovered that making antibodies that can find and attach to cancer cells in the body, and not to normal cells as well, is very difficult. Scientists have had limited successes to date.

In the 1970s and 1980s, scientists hoped that interferons, natural substances produced by the body that work by boosting the activity of the immune system, would provide the answer to cancer. In 1986, interferon became the first biological agent licensed by the United States federal government for cancer therapy. Interferons, however, have been mostly disappointing, with only a few successes against some rare cancers, such as hairy-cell leukemia and Kaposi's sarcoma.

In the late 1980s, a natural cancer-fighting substance called interleukin-2 was thought to have anticancer properties, but it has often proven to be very dangerous when given to patients in large amounts. Scientists at the NCI have been testing interleukin together with a vaccine against some types of cancer.

Today, researchers continue to try a number of strategies to fight cancer using the body's own weapons. They are using biologic agents to alert the immune system to a cancer, boosting the body's number of cancer-fighting cells and arming these cells with cancer toxins to attempt to destroy the cancer. They are attaching substances to the cancer cells themselves to make tumors alert the immune system and trigger an attack.

Alternative Therapies

Some patients and occasionally even a few doctors use alternative therapies to treat cancer. Alternative medicine is made up of treatments that are unproven because they have not been scientifically tested, or were tested and found to have little effectiveness. These are different from investigational treatments, which are treatments that are being tested scientifically. Many alternative therapies are promoted by individuals who are not medical doctors.

Alternative treatments are really more accurately called complementary treatments. They are meant to be taken in addition to, and not instead of, mainstream treatments. Some of these include acupuncture, stress management, biofeedback, and various herbal remedies. These therapies do not cure patients; rather, they attempt to control symptoms and improve the patients' well-being.

Thousands of Americans are trying alternative treatments for different reasons. But for those with cancer, one reason stands out: Unless the disease is found early, most mainstream treatments cannot promise a cure. Many alternative therapies offer hope. Many patients do not believe in miracle cures but still try alternative medicine to improve their quality of life.[10]

Many doctors worry about unwarranted claims by those who promote alternative medicines and are concerned that some patients might take such treatments instead of the conventional, standard therapy. Still, researchers are finding that some therapies such as acupuncture and stress reduction actually help relieve some symptoms. Because of alternative medicine's increasing appeal, the federal government, through the National Institutes of Health, established an Office of Alternative Medicine in 1992 to investigate some of the most promising practices. In the past few years, many medical schools and hospitals have opened centers or departments to scientifically study complementary medicine.

What Is a Clinical Trial?

Clinical trials are very important for medicine to progress. When researchers want to evaluate a new, promising treatment, they usually conduct a clinical trial. The clinical trial is one of the final stages of a long, careful research process. After laboratory and animal testing, a new treatment needs to be proven safe and effective in a certain number of patients before it can be made widely available. It is hoped that the new treatment will be a marked improvement over the old.

A trial usually tests a new drug, a new approach to surgery or radiation treatment, a different combination of these treatments, or a totally new technique such as gene therapy. The results of the trial are compared with the standard treatment results. The standard treatment is the best treatment currently known. The group of patients who receive the standard treatment is called the control group.

One of the concerns in doing clinical trials is patient or doctor bias affecting results. One of the ways around this problem is a process called randomization. Patients are selected by chance to be put into one trial group or another. Neither the doctors nor the patients know which treatment is best, and who is receiving it. This is called a double-blind study.

The National Cancer Institute alone sponsors clinical trials on more than two hundred fifty anticancer agents. Clinical trials are part of a long, slow, often expensive process intended to improve standard treatments. It typically takes up to fourteen years and 70 million dollars for a new drug to become established as a standard treatment.[11]

Clinical trials involve some risk. Patients volunteer for a number of reasons, especially because they may be among the first to receive the latest effective drug. Often, patients volunteer because standard treatments offer little hope. While patients are free to leave a clinical trial at any time, many stay in the hope that they will benefit from the treatment. Some remain in a trial because they want to contribute to general medical knowledge and may be helping others.

7
Living with Cancer

Author Diana Burgwyn was visiting a family member in late summer 1993, when she accidentally ate a bowl of farina. Burgwyn, fifty-seven, had a terrible wheat allergy. Surprised that she had not suffered an allergic attack from the food, she went directly to her allergist. During the exam, the allergist asked Burgwyn about a lump on her neck and suggested that she see an ear, nose, and throat specialist.

A test revealed a throat nodule, which the doctor removed and biopsied. Burgwyn had thyroid cancer, and it had spread to her lymph nodes. After surgery and a treatment with radioactive iodine, the cancer disappeared. Some forms of thyroid cancer are easily treated. Every year Burgwyn returns to her doctor for an X ray to make sure the cancer has not returned. She also must take synthetic thyroid pills for the rest of her life. "I hardly think about it anymore," she said, "because it was so treatable."[1]

More than 8 million Americans alive today have had cancer. Cancer experts note a major change in the ways we regard cancer. Many years ago, our parents and grandparents would often refer to cancer as the "Big C." No one wanted to talk about it with family and friends because most of the time those with cancer died. But in the last two decades, marked improvements in treatment, diagnosis, prevention, and our basic understanding of how cancer develops and spreads has made cancer a topic to talk about in public. Doctors and patients discuss their disease and the treatment options much more openly today than they did in the past. This change began in the 1950s, when cancer chemotherapy began proving successful, often in combination with surgery and radiation. More than one half of all cancer patients now live for at least five years after diagnosis. Cancer is increasingly seen as a manageable, chronic disease.

Today's improved drug treatments make it less likely that cancer will return, allowing more patients than ever before to be at home instead of in the hospital. New anticancer drugs have become available in the past five years, including the drug Taxol for ovarian and breast cancer. Taxol can be given to patients who come to the hospital but do not stay overnight.

Better-Informed Patients

Americans today are taking a bolder attitude toward cancer than they did twenty years ago. While most patients used to simply accept a doctor's diagnosis, patients today are not satisfied to be passive consumers. Part of this resulted from the women's rights and consumer-rights movements in the 1960s. They began demanding more information and taking more responsibility for their own care. In the mid-1970s, first lady Betty Ford and Happy Rockefeller, wife of Vice-President Nelson Rockefeller, put cancer in the public view by talking about their own struggles with breast cancer.[2] Another reason for the new patient attitude is that there is much more information available about cancer in bookstores and libraries, in newspapers and magazines, and on television and the Internet. Many support groups, such as the National Coalition for Cancer Survivorship, have a national following.

"People—women in particular—often say, 'I want to have control of my life,'" says Matthew Loscalzo, director of patient and family services at Johns Hopkins Oncology Center in Baltimore. The physical, emotional, and spiritual health of the patient need to be considered. "Psychological care has a role in every part of the cancer experience. There is no treatment of cancer that feels good, and no treatment that doesn't affect some important aspect of the patient's life," he points out.[3]

"The first reaction is dread, fear, and shock," explains Joan Hermann, director of social work services at Fox Chase Cancer Center, talking about patients' initial reactions to the news that they have cancer. "Most people ask, 'How could it happen to me?'"[4]

Cancer affects the entire family. Patients and families need support and encouragement. Cancer is a serious illness, and it is scary because no one knows if the person who has it will get well or not. It is also an upsetting illness, because many aspects of a patient's life will change. "If a parent has cancer, it is important to explain the cancer to their children, and how the illness will affect them," Hermann says. Families confronting cancer have to expect and deal with changes in responsibilities. "If mom is sick, dad and the grandparents often take on new roles, whether it be taking the child to school or cooking dinner, for example. It is natural that some family members will be upset with the extra chores, and actually begin to resent the added responsibilities."[5]

Doctors, nurses, social workers, and other health care specialists work with families in helping them manage the disease and the effects it may have on their lives.

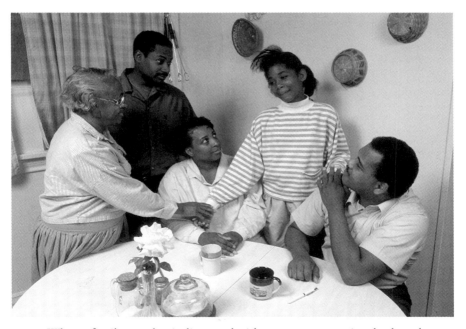

When a family member is diagnosed with cancer, everyone involved needs to understand and discuss the changes that may occur in their lives.

When Someone in Your Family Has Cancer

If a parent, brother, or sister has cancer, things may change. Someone different may drive you to band practice or make dinner. You may have to do some extra things around the house, like taking out the trash or mowing the lawn. You may have to stay home sometimes with your brother or sister.

People in your family may react differently. Some may feel sorry for the sick person. Others may be angry for the changes in their lives. They may be tense and not easy to talk to

Cure and Remission

It is important to understand the difference between a cure and a remission. Sometimes, cancer cells are destroyed and all symptoms and signs of disease vanish. The cancer is said to be in remission. That does not necessarily mean the cancer is completely gone but that doctors cannot find any evidence of it. A remission can be complete or partial. Partial means that only some of the signs and symptoms are gone. Doctors hesitate to use the term *cured* until a patient's disease has been in remission long enough that they feel certain it will not come back. The point at which a person is declared cured depends on the type of cancer. If the cancer returns, it is said to "relapse."

Sometimes, patients—children in particular—who are cured of one cancer have a greater chance than others to develop another type of cancer years later. This depends on the type of cancer these people originally had and the type of treatment they received.

because they are worried about the future. Treating cancer can be a long and tiring process for everyone. It is good for you to continue going to school and doing outside activities. You can talk with a family friend, priest, teacher, counselor, or doctor if you are worried or would like to find out more about cancer. The list of organizations in the "For More Information" section at the back of the book may also help you contact specialists.

Also remember that a person who has cancer will not necessarily die from it. Cancer is not contagious; you cannot catch it or give it to anyone. Nothing you did or did not do caused your family member to get cancer, and there was nothing you could have done to prevent your family member from getting it.

What Is It Like to Have Cancer?

Because each cancer is different and affects different parts of the body, no two cancers feel the same. Very often, people with cancer do not have any pain, at least not early in the disease. In breast and testicular cancers, for example, the early signs are painless lumps in the breast and the testicle. People with brain cancer may have problems focusing their attention or writing their name. But cancer can hurt. In 1998, New York Yankee star Darryl Strawberry had terrible stomach pains and was diagnosed with colon cancer. Some people with brain tumors have terrible headaches. Sometimes, the treatment side effects may be more uncomfortable or hurt worse than the disease.

Sometimes, people are treated unfairly when they have cancer or have survived the disease. Some employers may be reluctant to give cancer survivors jobs because they are worried that they will get sick again. For the same reason, it may also be difficult for people with cancer to get health insurance.

Cure Rates

In many cases, a person who is alive five years after getting cancer and shows no signs of the disease is considered cured. Yet *cured* is a term most cancer specialists avoid. Although they would like to be able to declare a person cured forever, they talk instead of survival rates, of the proportion of people who show no signs of disease for some years following treatment.

Millions of Americans have cancer, and many have very busy, full lives. It is important to remember to continue to do the things you enjoy.

Most cancers, if they are going to return, come back within five years, experts say. If someone is disease free for five years, this means that the odds are the cancer has been cured. An exception is breast cancer, which sometimes returns after as long as twenty years.

Why talk in odds, rates, and risks? Cancer is much more complex than a curable bacterial infection. Such illnesses tend to have a single cause. Cancer, on the other hand, often involves several steps of genetic alterations. Each step can affect the person in a different way, and each type of cancer can vary in its pattern.

For this reason, most experts say that finding one treatment for all cancers is pretty unlikely. A magic bullet to cure cancer, researchers agree, is not the goal today. Rather, they seek a custom-made plan to outsmart the particular ways certain cancers grow.

8

Preventing Cancer

When molecular biologist Howard Temin accepted a Nobel Prize in 1975 in Stockholm, Sweden, for his research in cancer biology, he had a message for the audience. He told the roomful of Scandinavian royalty and other dignitaries that while he hoped that his research would someday improve the understanding of cancer, there was something that people could do about cancer right now: Stop smoking.

Many in the audience nervously put out their cigarettes.

Temin, who did not smoke, was known for speaking out about the hazards of tobacco. Yet in 1994, Temin, at the age of fifty-nine, died of lung cancer.[1]

Temin's case of lung cancer was fairly unusual, because only one in seven lung cancers appears in nonsmokers. Preventing cancer is not easy; cancer so often seems beyond a person's control. However, many experts predict that the greatest turnaround in fighting cancer will come in prevention, rather than in new treatments. Some scientists believe that rather than spending millions on finding new cancer treatments, which is a long, often frustrating process, the government should devote millions of dollars to prevention and education programs.[2]

Doctors say that the best way to deal with cancer is to simply avoid its causes in the first place. Cigarette smoking, for example, is a very preventable cause of cancer, making lung cancer a preventable disease. People who do not smoke are much less likely to get cancer. Yet smoking alone is often not enough to cause cancer. About 85 percent of smokers

Cancer Prevention

The American Cancer Society recommends these ways to avoid cancer:

- Stay away from tobacco and too much sun.
- If you drink alcohol, do so in moderation.
- Avoid potentially cancer-causing substances, such as asbestos, at work.
- Eat a diet low in fat.
- Eat more fruit, vegetables, and fiber.
- Exercise to maintain a healthy weight.
- Avoid unnecessary X rays.
- Perform periodic self-examinations, especially of the skin, breasts, or testicles.

never get lung cancer, though they may have other illnesses such as heart disease.

Routine Self-Examinations

One of the most basic ways to look for signs of cancer is to perform self-examinations. Some tumors can be felt through the skin. The ACS recommends that women perform monthly self-examinations of their breasts.[3] They can then let their doctors know if they feel a change or a lump in their breasts. Men are encouraged to perform self-examinations of their testicles.

Scientists and other experts believe that regular exercise is one part of a healthy lifestyle that may prevent cancer.

Warts or moles that change color or grow may be signs of melanoma, a potentially deadly skin cancer that can be treated if found early. These are common, and the newspapers and television news frequently report athletes and celebrities who have cancerous moles removed in quick, easy procedures.[4]

Screening Tests

Several types of screening tests are available for people to catch early signs of, and in some cases, prevent, cancer. Both the National Cancer Institute and the American Cancer Society recommend that women, beginning at age forty, get a mammography screening annually to test for tissue changes that may indicate breast cancer.[5]

Those who are in favor of routine screening for prostate cancer recommend that healthy men older than fifty have both a rectal exam, in which a doctor can feel an enlarged prostate through the rectum, and PSA testing annually.[6]

The battle against colon cancer, a major killer in the United States, may be the most winnable, according to many oncologists. Many researchers are optimistic about colon cancer because of the advances in detecting and diagnosing the disease when it is still treatable. Some cases of colon cancer may be prevented. Polyps, growths in the lining of the colon, usually appear before colon cancer does. Removing these growths may greatly reduce the chance of developing cancer.

Looking in samples of bowel movements for blood may be one way to find large polyps or a newly developing cancer. Because polyps sometimes bleed, tests known as fecal occult blood tests, which detect blood or the breakdown products of blood in the feces, are useful to detect polyps that can signify cancer. Even better, colonoscopy and sigmoidoscopy, provide views of the colon by the insertion into the colon of a long, lighted tube with a tiny camera at the end.[7]

A Pap smear is one of the most accurate tests used to detect—and prevent—cervical cancer. It involves removing cells from a woman's cervix and examining them under a microscope. Slight changes in the cells may be early signs of cervical cancer.

Chemoprevention

Many cancer specialists suggest that the relatively young field of chemoprevention may play a great role in preventing cancer. Chemoprevention supporters believe that some substances—certain foods, drugs, and vitamins, for example—can actually prevent or reduce the chances of a person's developing cancer.[8]

Perhaps the most recent—and best—example of chemoprevention is the antiestrogen drug tamoxifen. Tamoxifen has been used for years to prevent breast cancer from returning. In 1992, the NCI decided to try to find out whether or not tamoxifen could actually prevent breast cancer in healthy women who were at high risk of developing the disease. It launched a 68-million-dollar study comparing women who were sixty or older, had a family history of breast cancer, or had precancerous breast lesions—all risk factors for breast cancer—who were randomly assigned to take tamoxifen, with others who were given a placebo, a dummy pill, for five years.

Tamoxifen appears to prevent the hormone estrogen from feeding a potentially developing cancer. Many cases of breast cancer depend on estrogen to grow.

In 1998, scientists announced very encouraging results. The study, called the Breast Cancer Prevention Trial, examined thirteen thousand women in the United States and Canada. It showed that tamoxifen reduced the chance of developing breast cancer in these high-risk women by 45 percent.[9] But there is a downside: those women who take tamoxifen have a higher than normal risk of developing uterine cancer.

Prevention can sometimes be a tricky thing. Cancer researchers often learn from negative trials—in other words, trials that did not quite measure up to expectations. That was the case with a prevention trial that ended in 1996. Because of promising results of earlier studies, scientists had assumed that a chemical called beta-carotene was useful in preventing lung cancer. A major prevention trial called the Beta-Carotene and Retinol Efficacy Trial, led by researchers at the Fred Hutchinson Cancer Research Center and University of Washington, was launched in 1985 to look at more than eighteen thousand men and women at high risk of lung cancer—from either heavy smoking or asbestos exposure. Half the subjects were given beta-carotene, which is present in many fruits and vegetables, and vitamin A supplements; the other half of the participants were given placebos.

But the study was stopped twenty-one months early. Preliminary results showed that the beta-carotene and vitamins gave no benefit to smokers, former smokers, or those who had been exposed to asbestos. In fact, the risk for lung cancer even increased for smokers receiving treatment.[10]

Researchers have no explanation for the increase, but it seems likely that substances other than beta-carotene are responsible for the protective effects of fruits and vegetables. Or perhaps beta-carotene is helpful in protecting against types of cancers other than those in the lungs, or in preventing cancers from returning a second time.

Foods and Cancers

Prevention, in some cases, means changing your habits or developing better habits. Let us look at diet, for example. When Mom tells you to eat all the vegetables on your plate, it is a good idea to listen to her. Eating the right foods can play an important role in cancer prevention. According to the NCI, eating a low-fat, high-fiber diet that is full of fruits, vegetables, and whole grains, as well as exercising and maintaining a healthy weight, helps reduce the chances of getting as many as one third of all cancers. These habits especially lower the risk of getting colon and stomach cancers.

Many fruits and vegetables—particularly cruciferous vegetables such as brussels sprouts, broccoli, and cabbage—actually contain cancer-fighting chemicals. Most nutrition and cancer experts maintain that people should eat at least five servings of fruits and vegetables daily, emphasizing citrus fruits for vitamin C and deep-yellow and dark-green vegetables for beta-carotene. Vitamins C and E and beta-carotene are antioxidants, which means they may help block cell damage caused by other dangerous, naturally occurring chemicals in your body called free radicals. Folic acid, a B vitamin, may block normal cells from becoming cancerous and strengthen the immune system.

Experts also recommend eating plenty of high-fiber grains and legumes, such as peas, beans, and lentils. Even garlic, which many people like to add to food, has anticancer properties.[11] High-fiber foods, such as whole grains, vegetables, and fruits, help prevent colon cancer. Dietary fiber includes a variety

Researchers say that a balanced diet containing plenty of fresh fruits and vegetables is one of the best ways to help prevent cancer.

of plant carbohydrates that people cannot digest. Fiber is either soluble or insoluble. Soluble fiber cuts the level of blood cholesterol; insoluble fiber, such as oat bran, may reduce the risk of colorectal cancer.

Foods rich in vitamin A, such as fresh carrots, apricots, squash, and broccoli, may protect against cancers of the larynx and esophagus. Foods containing vitamin C, including oranges, cantaloupes, lemons, strawberries, red and green peppers, broccoli, and tomatoes may protect against stomach and esophageal cancers.

At the same time, the ACS says that people should lower the amount of fat they eat. High-fat diets contribute to colon, breast, and prostate cancers. Doctors and nutritionists recommend that instead of indulging in fatty foods, everyone should eat low-fat dairy products, lean meat, fish, and poultry without skin. Diet and cancer experts also recommend staying away from salt-cured, smoked, and nitrate-cured foods, such as hot dogs and cold cuts. These may contribute to cancers of the esophagus and stomach.

On the Horizon: Research and the Future

Cancer is most dangerous when it spreads through organs in the body. When *USA Today* reporter Cathy Haines was diagnosed with advanced breast cancer that had spread to other parts of her body, in January 1998, she began treatments with the drug Taxol as part of a clinical trial at Georgetown University in Washington, D.C. Taxol was originally developed from the bark of the Pacific yew tree, but now scientists can manufacture the substance in the laboratory, greatly increasing the available supply.

When Haines began her Taxol treatment, doctors were not sure how well the drug worked against advanced breast cancer. Much of the tumor did shrink. The next step, the doctors and Haines decided, was to have breast surgery.[1]

Haines's clinical trial is one of 115 nationwide for women with advanced breast cancer. She has since begun a treatment course of the standard cancer drug Adriamycin. She will eventually take the chemotherapy drug cyclophosphamide.

Haines, who chronicled her struggle with cancer on the pages of *USA Today*, wants to get rid of her disease, or in cancer lingo, to become a complete responder, a person whose advanced disease no longer can be detected and whose treatment appears to be working. Doctors rarely talk about cures for women like Haines, whose cancer has spread to so much of her body. In the meantime, Haines and her fiancé postponed their wedding plans until her condition is more certain.[2]

While scientists and doctors in the last two decades have developed new and improved drugs against cancer, many more remain unproven.

Many scientists agree on two things when asked about fighting cancer in the future: First, prevention will be more important than ever, as improvements in medicines, surgery, and other treatments are slow to come along. Second, a key to finding better treatments for cancer lies in a greater understanding of how cancer begins and behaves. The more that scientists learn about the underlying genetic nature of cancer, the brighter the future will be.

Molecular Biology

The newest weapons in the war on cancer, and the ones scientists are confident will ultimately lead to triumph, lie in the field of molecular biology. The war on cancer took several large steps forward in the past few years with the discovery of new genes, many of which play roles in the development of

The Pacific yew tree is a source of the powerful cancer drug, Taxol. Taxol has been useful in treating ovarian and breast cancers.

cancer. Efforts continue through the NCI and the National Human Genome Research Institute and the Human Genome Project, the federal government's fifteen-year, 3-billion-dollar effort to locate and understand all human genes.

As a result, some scientists are taking advantage of the new understanding of molecular genetics and the cancer cell. For example, Frederica Perrera, a scientist and professor of environmental health at the Columbia School of Public Health in New York, looks for biological signs of cancer in the blood of people who have a very high cancer risk. She and her colleagues in a new field called molecular epidemiology explore how the body deals with potentially cancer-causing substances in the environment, such as cigarette smoke, chemical dyes, and solvents, and how they affect genes and contribute to cancer.[3]

Recent findings by molecular epidemiologists suggest that a particular person may be especially sensitive to one carcinogen, while another has no effect—depending on a particular combination of genes the person inherits. A man may smoke two packs of cigarettes a day for twenty years without getting lung cancer if he inherits a gene that protects against cigarette smoke. At the same time, another man who does not smoke and inherits a gene that makes him particularly sensitive to cigarette smoke may develop lung cancer just from constantly being around secondhand smoke.[4]

Such genes are called polymorphic genes, meaning that people can inherit a good form of a gene that reduces the odds of getting a cancer, or they can inherit a bad form, which could increase the likelihood of cancer. (Genes are inherited in pairs.) As researchers continue to identify such genes, molecular epidemiologists predict that within a decade they will be able to tell people which carcinogens present the greatest personal risk to them, essentially creating "cancer risk profiles."[5]

In another promising area, researcher David Sidransky of Johns Hopkins Oncology Center in Baltimore studies chemicals called microsatellites, which are small pieces of repeated genetic material. Sidransky's work shows that missing groups of microsatellites indicate missing genes and various genetic changes, possibly cancer.[6]

Gene Therapy

Some scientists are exploring the use of gene therapy against cancer. In fact, of more than two hundred gene therapy trials ongoing in the United States, roughly three quarters focus on cancer.

Gene therapy is a very experimental form of treatment for disease. The general idea is to attempt to replace a malfunctioning gene in cells. This has been very difficult to do, especially in the case of cancer because many genes are involved in causing cancer.

A promising clinical trial begun by scientists in Texas and California aims to actually fix damaged genes. According to an article in the *Wall Street Journal,* three companies are testing gene therapy in patients.[7] Earlier experiments in the test tube showed that putting p53 into cancer cells stopped cell division. In 1996, scientists also demonstrated that they could place p53, using a modified virus, into animal cancer cells and stop tumors from growing. Many drug makers and scientists believe that gene therapy cannot be done in large enough amounts to work in cancer, or cannot work without harmful side effects. Still, scientists at the three companies are attempting to insert the p53 gene into cancer cells and have begun testing the therapy on patients.

Another type of cancer gene therapy aims to deliver cancer-killing agents, in combination with other products, directly to the tumor. One international clinical trial, for example, tests the idea of inserting "suicide genes" inside a brain tumor. It works like this: A gene from a type of herpesvirus is chemically inserted inside tumor cells. The cells then carry virus DNA, which, in turn, is sensitive to the antiviral drug ganciclovir. When doctors give patients ganciclovir, the drug attacks the cells. Most studies are still in the early stages, however, and although they are promising, they have had limited success to date.

Antiangiogenesis Drugs

At first, few believed Judah Folkman when he and his co-workers suggested that for tumors to grow, they needed a blood supply. Without this process, called angiogenesis, they would die. Today, it is one of the hottest areas of cancer research.

In February 1997, Folkman and his coworkers announced a new drug called endostatin, which had been successful in stopping angiogenesis in animal studies. It could take a decade or more of testing in people before this drug could become available, however, and only patients with advanced cancer who have not responded to other treatments will be able to participate in trial studies.[8]

Now, it appears that Folkman and his colleagues are even closer to finding an answer to the problem. In May 1998, they announced that within a year, if all goes well, the first cancer patient will be injected with two new drugs that potentially can eliminate any type of cancer, with no obvious side effects and no drug resistance. At least, that is the case so far in mice, the usual animals used to test cancer drugs. The two drugs, angiostatin and endostatin, are not typical anticancer drugs, which work against the cancer. Instead, these drugs work by interfering with the blood supply that tumors need. Given together, they make tumors in mice disappear and not return.[9]

Antitelomerase Drugs

Telomeres are the protective caps of chromosomes. They play important roles in determining the length of cell division and cell life. Recent findings by scientists show that telomeres may also be involved in cancer. Eventually, as cells get old, telomeres fray, and cell division becomes haphazard and unreliable, causing cells to die. But when this system breaks down, a mutation in the DNA causes the cell to make telomerase, an enzyme that repairs and maintains telomeres. Cells continue to divide. Somehow, some scientists believe, the cancer cell is able to restore telomerase, interfering with the normal aging of the cell.[10] Some studies by researchers at Geron Corp., in Menlo Park, California, working on ovarian cancer, think that blocking telomerase from working may be a way of fighting cancer.

Cancer Vaccines

In 1996, Adele Fiel, a suburban New Jersey grandmother, began having abdominal pains and fatigue. After complaining of not feeling well, she saw her doctor and was diagnosed with late-stage ovarian cancer. Ovarian cancer is very difficult to diagnose early because its symptoms are so vague.

Surgery failed to remove the entire cancer, and she received several different chemotherapy drugs. The cancer proved difficult to control. One doctor convinced her to freeze some of her tumor cells for later research study. It proved a very good idea.

A short time later, Fiel underwent a second surgery and another round of chemotherapy. In the meantime, her son, a prominent Philadelphia lawyer, heard about a promising cancer vaccine being developed in Philadelphia. David Berd, a medical oncologist at the Kimmel Cancer Center at Thomas Jefferson University, had spent a decade searching for the right formula for such a vaccine. In Berd's vaccine, the patient's own tumor cells are mixed with a chemical, dinitrophenyl, to make the tumor appear more foreign to the body, paving the way for the immune system to chase down and destroy cancer cells.

Though her visible cancer was removed, Fiel's doctor had frozen cells earlier, cells now needed to make Berd's vaccine. "No one has ever given me a guarantee," Fiel said. "I certainly wouldn't give anyone one." As of March 1998, after a year of vaccine treatments, her cancer was in remission. "It's hard not to be preoccupied with your cancer. I try not to let it be the center of my life. I always felt that I would survive."[11]

In theory, vaccines work by stimulating the body's immune system to overcome foreign invaders. Cancer vaccines are an exciting but very new area of research. Though the notion of a cancer vaccine has been around for about one hundred years, actually inventing one has been quite a different story. Current versions of vaccines are different from the vaccines children typically receive. Those vaccines prevent illnesses such as measles, mumps, and a number of other diseases. But cancer is not so simple. It cannot be prevented with just a shot. Instead, vaccines are used in addition to the usual treatments that may include, among other things, surgery, radiation, and drugs. Cancer vaccines are aimed at preventing cancer from returning, and in some cases, they are designed to remove cancer in people who already have it. Like their counterparts against mumps and whooping cough, they work by summoning the body's immune defenses.

Vaccines come in two main varieties. The first is called a tailored vaccine. It is made separately for each patient and is constructed from cells from the patient's tumor. A generic vaccine, in contrast, takes advantage of single substances called antigens that are shared by many or most patients with a

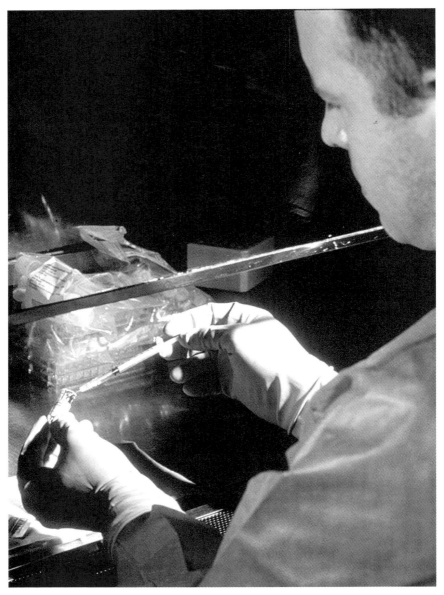

Promising new treatments such as cancer vaccines are designed to use the body's immune system to fight cancer.

particular type of cancer. In theory, large numbers of these patients may be treated this way.

Several different versions of cancer vaccines are now being tested in clinical trials across the nation. Berd's tailored vaccine has been one of the most successful. In his initial clinical trials, Berd has seen nearly 60 percent of 150 malignant melanoma patients live for five years or more. This is a remarkable success rate. The vaccine is now in larger, Phase III clinical trials to see whether it works in a larger group of patients.

Steven Rosenberg, chief of surgery at the NCI and a pioneer in the development of cancer vaccines, has seen promising results with a type of vaccine involving interleukin-2 (IL-2), a protein produced by the body that helps activate various immune cells. Rosenberg altered proteins on the surface of the melanoma cancer cell, then injected thirty-one advanced melanoma patients with interleukin-2. In 42 percent of the patients given the vaccine-IL-2 combination, tumors shrank. Only 17 percent of the patients who received IL-2 alone showed response.[12]

New Programs

Several national programs, based at the NCI and the ACS, are aimed at improving our understanding of the nature of cancer. The NCI's Cancer Gene Anatomy Project, for example, will allow scientists to ultimately understand each person's cancer. The project is designed to explain the precise patterns of genetic changes that determine how a   particular cancer behaves, including how it grows, whether it will spread, and whether certain treatments will work. This information could help researchers find better ways to detect, diagnose, treat, and prevent cancer.

Many doctors and scientists see a bright future in the battle against cancer. As they continue to learn more about how cancer develops, they will create new drugs and devise new ways to deal with the disease.

Q & A

Q. If my uncle and father have cancer, does that mean that I will get it, too?

A. No, not necessarily. Many factors determine whether a person develops cancer. Heredity is only one. Lifestyle choices, such as diet, tobacco use, and sun exposure, contribute, as do environmental exposures, many unknown factors, and chance.

Q. Can I catch cancer?

A. Cancer is genetic; you cannot catch it like a cold. It results from damage to genes. A number of things may contribute to this damage, such as diet, radiation, smoking, sunburn, and viruses. Viruses, which people can acquire from others, may actually play a large role in the development of some cancers, such as cervical and liver cancers.

Q. I heard that people worry about living near electrical lines. Is that a problem?

A. No; several recent studies by the NCI have disproved any claims about dangers of developing cancer from living near power lines and electromagnetic fields.

Q. Do artificial sweeteners cause cancer?

A. Some experiments in rats years ago showed a link between saccharin and cancer. However, more recent studies of primates and humans have not proven any increased risk from either saccharin or aspartame.

Q. What is dietary fiber, and can it prevent cancer?

A. Dietary fiber includes a variety of plant carbohydrates not digested by humans. High-fiber foods include grains and legumes, such as peas, beans, and lentils. Fiber is either soluble or insoluble. Soluble fiber cuts the level of blood cholesterol; insoluble fiber is thought to reduce the risk of colorectal cancer.

Q. If genes determine cancer risk, how can diet prevent cancer?

A. Genes that increase or decrease cancer risk may be inherited, whereas others may be changed or damaged throughout life. Nutrients and nutritional factors from food can protect the DNA from damage and possibly delay or prevent cancer development. Moreover, risk is not the same as having the disease.

Q. Is there a vaccine for cancer?

A: Though some are promising, they remain experimental. Cancer vaccines are different from typical vaccines. Traditional vaccines work by preventing illnesses caused by viruses, such as the flu and measles. Because most cancers do not develop from infectious agents such as viruses, a vaccine to prevent cancer has not yet turned out to be very useful.

Cancer Timeline

2500 B.C.— Egyptians first describe cancer, and later perform
–1600 B.C. crude cancer surgery.

400 B.C.— The Greek physician Hippocrates coins the term
carcinoma from *karkinos*, the ancient Greek word
for "crab."

1775— London physician Percivall Pott documents
scrotal cancer in young boys who clean
chimneys, the first recognized example of an
environmentally caused cancer.

1911— A viral cause of cancer in chickens is documented
by Peyton Rous, leading to later discoveries by
researchers about the roles of genes in cancer.

1913— The American Society for the Control of Cancer
is established to educate the public about cancer.

1915— Scientists prove chemicals could cause cancer.

1937— Congress passes the National Cancer Institute
Act, authorizing annual funding to support
cancer research through a National Cancer
Institute.

1964— United States Surgeon General C. Everett Koop
issues a report warning about the connection
between cigarette smoking and lung cancer.

1971— President Richard M. Nixon and the United
States government declare war on cancer by
signing into law the National Cancer Act.

1975—Scientists, led by J. Michael Bishop and Harold Varmus discover that a defective gene that causes cancer in chickens is nearly identical to a human gene. This led to the conclusion that cells become cancerous because the normal genetic machinery somehow does not work correctly. The scientists, along with Robert Weinberg, begin describing oncogenes, or cancer-causing genes.

1980s—Scientists describe tumor-suppressor genes, the normally protective genes that halt cell growth. In cancer, they malfunction. Researchers identify the first tumor-suppressor gene, Rb, which, when altered, causes retinoblastoma, a rare eye cancer.

1990s—Researchers identify and isolate a tumor-suppressor gene—BRCA1—for breast cancer. Though it is a rare cause of breast cancer, when the gene malfunctions, women have as much as an 85 percent risk of developing the disease. A damaged BRCA1 may be responsible for about 25 percent of all breast cancers in women under age thirty.

For More Information

American Association for Cancer Research
Public Ledger Building, Suite 816
150 S. Independence Mall West
Philadelphia, PA 19106-3483
215-440-9300
Fax: 215-440-9313
E-mail: webmaster@aacr.org
http://www.aacr.org

American Cancer Society
1599 Clifton Road NE
Atlanta, GA 30329-4251
800-227-2345
http://www.cancer.org

American Society of Clinical Oncology
225 Reinekers Lane, Suite 650
Alexandria, VA 22314
703-299-0150
Fax: 703-299-1044
E-mail: asco@asco.org
http://www.asco.org

National Cancer Institute
Office of Cancer Communications
31 Center Drive MSC 2580
Building 31, Room 10A19
Bethesda, MD 20892-2580
800-4-CANCER
http://www.nci.nih.gov

The National Alliance of Breast Cancer Organizations (NABCO)
9 East Thirty-seventh Street, 10th floor
New York, NY 10016
888-80NABCO
Fax: 212-689-1213
E-mail: NABCOinfo@aol.com
http://www.nabco.org

Chapter Notes

Chapter 1. Cancer: An Old Foe Begins to Reveal Its Secrets

1. John Hastings, "Wishing on a Fallen Star," *Health*, September 1993, p. 68.

2. Ibid.

3. Steven I. Benowitz, "Are We Winning the War on Cancer?" *The World Book Health and Medical Annual*, 1996, pp. 228–230.

4. Sheryl Gay Stolberg, "New Cancer Cases Decreasing in U.S. as Deaths Do, Too," *The New York Times*, March 13, 1998, pp. A1, A14; *American Cancer Society Cancer Facts and Figures—1998* (Atlanta, Ga.: American Cancer Society, 1998).

5. *American Cancer Society Cancer Facts and Figures—1998*.

6. National Cancer Advisory Board, National Cancer Institute, September 1994.

Chapter 2. A History of Cancer

1. National Cancer Institute, *Closing in on Cancer: Solving a 5000-Year-Old Mystery* (Bethesda, Md.: National Institutes of Health Publication Number 98-2955, 1998), pp. 3–5.

2. National Cancer Institute, "A Pictorial History of the National Cancer Institute," *History of the National Cancer Institute*, n.d., <http://rex.nci.nih.gov/wlcm/NCI_History/html/pictorial_intro.html> (January 22, 1999).

3. *Closing in on Cancer: Solving a 5000-Year-Old Mystery*, p. 4.

4. Ibid., p. 9.

5. Ibid., p. 20.

6. Samuel Hellman and Everett E. Vokes, "Advancing Current Treatments for Cancer," *Scientific American*, September 1996, p. 119.

7. National Cancer Institute.

8. *Closing in on Cancer: Solving a 5000-Year-Old Mystery*, p. 24.

9. Robert Langreth, "Arsenal of Hope: Revolution in Genetics Arms Cancer Fighters with Potent Weapons," *Wall Street Journal*, May 6, 1998, pp. A1, A12.

10. Ibid., p. A12.

11. Robert A. Weinberg, "How Cancer Arises," *Scientific American*, September 1996, pp. 62–63.

12. Ibid.

Chapter 3. What Is Cancer?

1. Gerald P. Murphy, Lois B. Morris, and Dianne Lange, *Informed Decisions: The Complete Book of Cancer Diagnosis, Treatment and Recovery* (New York: American Cancer Society/Viking Penguin, 1997), p. 15.

2. Ibid.

3. Dimitrios Trichopoulos, Frederick Li, and David J. Hunter, "What Causes Cancer?" *Scientific American*, September 1996, p. 81.

4. Murphy, Morris, and Lange, p. 82.

5. Robert Langreth, "Arsenal of Hope: Revolution in Genetics Arms Cancer Fighters With Potent Weapons," *Wall Street Journal*, May 6, 1998, pp. A1, A12.

6. Trichopoulos, Li, and Hunter, pp. 82–83.

7. Webster K. Caveniee et al., "Genetic Origins of Mutations Predisposing to Retinoblastoma", *Science*, 1985, vol. 228, no. 4698, pp. 501–503.

8. Richard Fishel et al., "The Human Mutator Gene Homologue MSH2 and its Association with Hereditary Nonpolyposis Colon Cancer Locus," *Cell*, December 1993, vol. 75, pp. 1027–1038.

9. Yoshio Miki et al., " A Strong Candidate for the Breast and Ovarian Cancer Susceptibility Gene BRCA1," *Science*, October 7, 1994, pp. 66–71; P. Andrew Futreal et al., "BRCA1 Mutations in Primary Breast and Ovarian Carcinomas," *Science*, October 7, 1997, pp. 120–122.

Chapter 4. Major Cancers

1. Jane E. Brody, "A Fatal Shift in Cancer's Gender Gap," *The New York Times*, May 12, 1998, p. F7.

2. Gerald P. Murphy, Lois B. Morris, and Dianne Lange, *Informed Decisions: The Complete Book of Cancer Diagnosis, Treatment and Recovery* (New York: American Cancer Society/Viking Penguin, 1997), pp. 477–647.

3. Lisa J. Bain, *A Parent's Guide to Childhood Cancer* (New York: Dell Publishing, 1995), pp. 11–22.

4. Scott Hamilton, "Fighting Heart," *People*, September 8, 1997, <http://www.pathfinder.com/People/970908/features/cover2.html> (December 1, 1998).

5. "Twelve Major Cancers," *Scientific American*, September 1996, pp. 126–132.

6. Bain, pp. 11–22.

7. D. Maxwell Parkin et al., "Estimates of the Worldwide Frequency of Sixteen Major Cancers in 1980," *International Journal of Cancer*, 1988, pp. 184–197.

8. Bain, pp. 11–22.

Chapter 5. Diagnosing Cancer

1. Author interview with Diana Burgwyn, May 3, 1998, Philadelphia, Pa.

2. Ibid.

3. Gerald P. Murphy, Lois B. Morris, and Dianne Lange, *Informed Decisions: The Complete Book of Cancer Diagnosis, Treatment and Recovery* (New York: American Cancer Society/Viking Penguin, 1997), pp. 24–25.

4. Ibid.

5. Ibid., p. 55.

6. Ibid., pp. 61–62.

7. Gerald E. Hanks and Peter T. Scardino, "Does Screening for Prostate Cancer Make Sense?" *Scientific American*, September 1996, pp. 114–115.

8. Murphy, Morris, and Lange, p. 66.

Chapter 6. Treating Cancer

1. Author interview with Tracy Newhall, April 3, 1998, Fox Chase Cancer Center, Philadelphia, Pa.

2. Ibid.

3. Ibid.

4. Ibid.

5. Author interview with Russell Schilder, April 3, 1998, Fox Chase Cancer Center, Philadelphia, Pa.

6. Ibid.

7. Robin Herman, "The New Weapons," *Washington Post/Health*, December 3, 1991, p. 14.

8. Steven I. Benowitz, "Are We Winning the War on Cancer?" *The World Book Health and Medical Annual*, 1996, pp. 226–241.

9. Kelli Whitlock, "Today's Radiation Therapy," *Frontiers*, October 1995, pp. 21–23.

10. Gerald P. Murphy, Lois B. Morris, and Dianne Lange, *Informed Decisions: The Complete Book of Cancer Diagnosis, Treatment and Recovery* (New York: American Cancer Society/Viking Penguin, 1997), pp. 239–245.

11. Ibid., pp. 228–238.

Chapter 7. Living with Cancer

1. Author interview with Diana Burgwyn, May 3, 1998, Philadelphia, Pa.

2. Tamar Lewin, "Changing View of Cancer: Something to Live With," *The New York Times*, February 4, 1991, pp. A1, B6.

3. Author interview with Matthew Loscalzo, March 16, 1998, Philadelphia, Pa.

4. Author interview with Joan Hermann, April 3, 1998, Fox Chase Cancer, Philadelphia, Pa.

5. Ibid.

Chapter 8. Preventing Cancer

1. Rick Weiss, "What's Your Cancer Profile," *Washington Post/Health*, September 19, 1995, p. 12.

2. Tim Beardsley, "A War Not Won," *Scientific American*, January 1994, pp. 135–136.

3. Gerald P. Murphy, Lois B. Morris, and Dianne Lange, *Informed Decisions: The Complete Book of Cancer Diagnosis, Treatment and Recovery* (New York: American Cancer Society/Viking Penguin, 1997), p. 50.

4. Ibid., p. 31.

5. American Cancer Society, *Mammography Guidelines*, March 1998.

6. Murphy, Morris, and Lange, pp. 46–47.

7. Mayo Clinic, "Cancer: What You Eat Can Affect Your Risk," *Mayo Clinic Health Letter,* September 1995; American Cancer Society, *Nutritional Guidelines,* 1996.

8. Murphy, Morris, and Lange, pp. 39–40.

9. Peter Greenwald, "Chemoprevention of Cancer," *Scientific American,* September 1996, pp. 96–99.

10. National Cancer Institute, press release, April 1998.

11. G. S. Omenn et al., "Effects of a Combination of Beta-Carotene and Vitamin A on Lung and Cardiovascular Disease," *New England Journal of Medicine,* May 2, 1996, vol. 334, no. 18, pp. 1150–1155.

Chapter 9. On the Horizon: Research and the Future

1. Tim Friend, "A Body Responding to Treatment," *USA Today,* March 26, 1998, p. 6D.

2. Ibid.

3. Steven Benowitz, "Molecular Advances Offer New Tools, New Hope for Cancer Studies," *The Scientist,* December 9, 1998, p. 17.

4. Rick Weiss, "What's Your Cancer Profile?" *Washington Post/Health,* September 19, 1995, p. 12.

5. Ibid., pp. 12–14.

6. Benowitz, p. 17.

7. Robert Langreth, "Arsenal of Hope: Revolution in Genetics Arms Cancer Fighters with Potent Weapons," *Wall Street Journal,* May 6, 1998, p. A12.

8. Faye Flam, "Cancer Theory Offers Hope for New Drugs to Starve Tumors," *Knight–Ridder Newspapers,* March 20, 1997.

9. Gina Kolata, "A Cautious Awe Greets Drugs That Eradicate Tumors in Mice," *The New York Times*, May 3, 1998, p. A1.

10. Robert S. Boyd, "Scientists May Have Found New Way to Fight Cancer by Blocking Substance That Allows Malignant Cells to Multiply," *Knight-Ridder/Tribune News Service*, April 11, 1994.

11. Author interview with Adele Fiel, March 2, 1998, Thomas Jefferson University, Philadelphia, Pa.

12. S. A. Rosenberg et al., "Immunologic and Therapeutic Evaluation of a Synthetic Peptide Vaccine for the Treatment of Patients with Metastatic Melanoma," *Nature Medicine*, March 1998, vol. 4, no. 3, pp. 321–327.

Glossary

antibodies—Proteins produced to attach specifically to foreign substances called antigens, such as surface antigens on a virus.

benign—Noncancerous.

biologics—Natural substances made in the body that affect the immune system's response to infection and tumors.

biopsy—Removal of a sample of tissue to see if cancer cells are present.

bone marrow—Soft tissue that occupies the cavities inside bone.

cancer—General term for more than one hundred diseases characterized by abnormal and uncontrolled growth of cells.

cancer cells—Cells present in malignant tissue.

carcinogen—Substance that increases the risk of cancer.

carcinoma—Cancer that develops in epithelial tissue, such as the lining of the lungs, liver, breasts, or colon. Up to 90 percent of cancers are carcinomas.

chemoprevention—Taking a drug to prevent cancer from developing.

chemotherapy—Treatment with anticancer drugs.

chromosome—Structure within the cell nucleus containing the genes.

clinical trial—Study designed to answer specific questions, often comparing a new untried treatment with the standard, which is the best treatment currently known.

colon—The large intestine, which extends from the end of the small intestine to the rectum.

colorectal—Refering to the colon and the rectum.

computed tomography (CT) imaging—Technique that uses X rays and a computer to produce cross-section views of the inside of the body.

DNA—Deoxyribonucleic acid. The molecule that encodes genetic information.

endoscope—Lighted, cylinder-shaped magnifying instrument.

gene—Length of DNA that carries the chemical information necessary for producing a protein. Genes are the basic units of heredity.

Hodgkin's disease—Cancer of the lymphatic system that produces enlarged lymph nodes, spleen, and liver.

immune system—The body's defense against invading germs.

immunotherapy—Treating disease by manipulating the body's immune system.

leukemia—Cancer of the bone marrow and lymph system.

lymph nodes—Small organs of the immune system where red and white blood cells are stored.

lymphoma—Cancer of the lymph nodes.

malignant—Cancerous.

malignant melanoma—Deadly type of skin cancer.

mammogram—X-ray test that looks for abnormalities in the tissue of the breast.

metastasis—Process by which cancer spreads in the body. Left unchecked, it can be deadly.

monoclonal antibody—Specific antibody made in the laboratory to home in on target cancer cells. It may be used in both cancer diagnosis and treatment.

oncogene—Altered gene that no longer controls cell growth properly. It usually plays an important role in causing cancer.

Pap smear—A cervical cancer screening test that involves the removal and examination of cells from a woman's cervix.

prostate—Walnut-shaped gland that lies at the base of the bladder in males. It provides a milky fluid that is important to producing semen.

proto-oncogene—A gene that has the potential to change into an active oncogene involved in causing cancer.

remission—A state in which cancer stops growing and its symptoms subside.

sarcoma—Cancer that arises from connective tissue such as bone, cartilage, or muscle. It may also affect the liver, lungs, spleen, kidneys, and bladder.

staging—Method used to classify tumors, depending on how likely they are to spread.

tumor—Any abnormal growth that may interfere with the growth of healthy tissue.

viruses—Very small organisms that can cause infection. Viruses survive only inside living cells.

X ray—High-energy radiation used at low levels to diagnose disease and at high levels to treat cancer.

Further Reading

Books

Bain, Lisa J. *A Parent's Guide to Childhood Cancer*. New York: Dell Publishing, 1995.

Gold, John C. *Cancer*. Parsippany, N.J.: Silver Burdett Press, 1997.

Gordon, Melanie A. *Let's Talk About When Kids Have Cancer*. New York: The Rosen Publishing Group, 1998.

Landau, Elaine. *Cancer*. New York: Twenty-First Century Books, Inc., 1995.

Warner, Gayle, and David Kreger. *Dancing at the Edge of Life: A Memoir*. New York: Hyperion, 1998.

Articles

Benowitz, Steven. "Molecular Advances Offer New Tools, New Hope for Cancer Studies." *The Scientist*, December 9, 1996, pp. 14, 17.

_____. "Are We Winning the War on Cancer?" *The World Book Health and Medical Annual*, 1996, pp. 226–241.

Cowley, Geoffrey. "Cancer and Diet." *Newsweek*, November 30, 1998, pp. 60–66.

Friend, Tim. "A Body Responding to Treatment." *USA Today*, March 26, 1998, p. 6D.

Greenwald, Peter. "Chemoprevention of Cancer." *Scientific American*, September 1996, pp. 96–99.

Holland, Jimmie C. "Cancer's Psychological Challenges." *Scientific American*, September 1996, pp. 158–161.

Laino, Charlotte. "Vaccines Seek, Destroy Melanomas." MSNBC, *Health News*, March 2, 1998.

Nash, J. Madeleine. "The Enemy Within." *Time*, Fall 1996, pp. 14–23.

Stolberg, Sheryl Gay. "New Cancer Cases Decreasing in the U.S., as Deaths Do Too." *The New York Times*, March 13, 1998, pp. A1, A14.

Trichopoulos, Dimitrios, Frederick P. Li, and David J. Hunter. "What Causes Cancer?" *Scientific American*, September 1996, pp. 80–87.

"Twelve Major Cancers." *Scientific American*, September 1996, pp. 126–132.

Weinberg, Robert A. "How Cancer Arises." *Scientific American*, September 1996, pp. 62–70.

Weiss, Rick. "What's Your Cancer Profile?" *Washington Post/Health*, September 19, 1995, pp. 12–14.

Wickelgren, Ingrid. "Cancer Vaccines." *Popular Science*, January 1998, pp. 63–68.

Internet Addresses

National Cancer Institute. "A Pictorial History of the National Cancer Institute," 1998. <http://rex.nci.nih.gov.>.

The Trustees of The University of Pennsylvania. *OncoLink®: University of Pennsylvania Cancer Center.* 1994–1999. <http://cancer.med.upenn.edu> (January 22, 1999).

NCCN. *National Comprehensive Cancer Center Network, Inc.®* 1998. <http://www.nccn.org/> (January 22, 1999).

Index